he Tel T

Léo Malet was born in Montpellier in 1909. He had no formal
education and began as a cabaret singer at 'La Vache enragée'
in Montmartre in 1925. He became an anarchist and
contributed to various magazines: *L'Insurgé, Journal de
l'Homme aux sandales* . . . He had various jobs: office worker,
ghost writer, manager of a fashion magazine, cinema extra,
newspaper seller . . .

From 1930 to 1940 he belonged to the Surrealist Group and
was a close friend of André Breton, René Magritte and Yves
Tanguy. During that time he published several collections of
poetry.

In 1943, inspired by the American writers Raymond Chandler
and Dashiel Hammett, he created Nestor Burma, the Parisian
private detective whose first mystery, *120 Rue de la Gare* was
an instant success and marked the beginning of a new era in
French detective fiction.

More than sixty novels were to follow over the next twenty
years. Léo Malet won the 'Grand Prix de l'humour noir' in 1958
for his series 'Les nouveaux mystères de Paris', each of which
is set in a different *arrondissement*. *The Tell-Tale Body on the
Plaine Monceau*, set in the 17th *arrondissement*, was first
published in 1959 as *L'envahissant cadavre de la plaine
Monceau*.

Léo Malet lives in Châtillon, just south of Paris.

30p

Other books by Léo Malet in Pan

Léo Malet

The Tell-Tale Body
on the Plaine Monceau
translated from the French by Peter Hudson
general editor: Barbara Bray

Pan Books
London, Sydney and Auckland

First published in France 1959 by Robert Laffont, Paris,
in the series *Nouveaux Mystères de Paris*

Published in France in 1987 by Editions Fleuve Noir
as *L'envahissant cadavre de la plaine Monceau*

This edition first published 1993 by Pan Books Ltd

a division of Pan Macmillan Publishers Limited
Cavaye Place London SW10 9PG
and Basingstoke

Associated companies throughout the world

ISBN 0 330 32867 0

9 8 7 6 5 4 3 2 1

A CIP catalogue record for this book is available from
the British Library

Phototypeset by Intype, London
Printed by Cox & Wyman Ltd, Reading, Berks

Contents

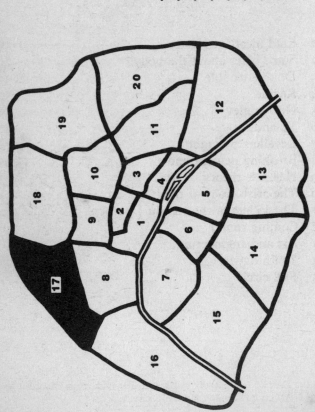

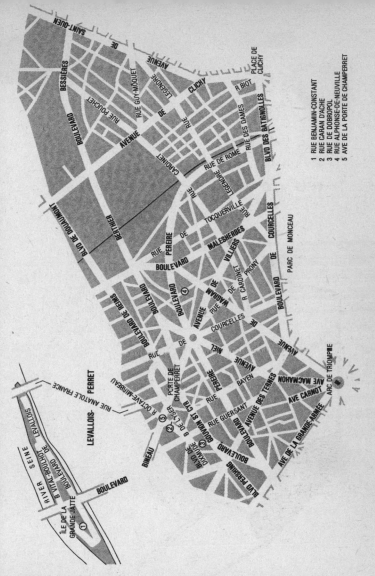

Plaine Monceau is a quartier in the 17th arrondissement. Monceau was a village that existed in the fourteenth century.

1 *Cold meat for Nestor*

I don't care what they say, you do get some lovely mornings in Paris in March. The morning I'm thinking about, for example. Spring was just around the corner – two weeks away, if the calendar was anything to go by – and though the weather would probably go to pot from then on, for the moment it was delightful. The trees were in bud down the avenue de Wagram; the breeze rustled gently through the branches. Everything nice and peaceful.

My watch said a quarter to nine.

Fifteen minutes to go before my appointment. I was meeting a woman who called herself Désiris. That couldn't be her real name, even if it was how she chose to appear in the telephone directory. (I'd checked.) It sounded like the kind of pseudonym a tart might use, or a certain class of pimp, or the manageress of a marriage bureau. But it was this hint of voluptuousness that had made me agree to see her when she phoned yesterday, though the yarn she'd tried to spin me had been both confusing and unconvincing.

I went into a café to pass the time.

When I came out again, the lower part of the avenue

de Wagram still wasn't exactly humming with activity. The early traffic was light enough to raise false hopes in motorists speeding towards the jams awaiting them up by the Arc de Triomphe. The broad pavements were almost empty, apart from a woman delivering bread, a street-cleaner leaning pensively on the handle of his broom, and a few concierges tidying up around the entrances to their courtyards. A glum-faced flunkey was taking an ugly and expensive-looking little pooch out for its constitutional.

On the balconies of opulent middle-class flats, house-maids with scarves round their heads shook dusters and beat carpets. They say the early bird catches the worm, but in Paris all he's likely to catch before ten in the morning is germs, breadcrumbs, household refuse, and various other unidentifiable flying objects.

The house I was heading for at this unearthly hour was a small private mansion in the middle of the rue Alphonse-de-Neuville which looked like a miniature castle out of an operetta. There are still quite a few of these villas around here, survivors of a bygone age when there were swarms of them, built as residences for stars of the Salon or the boudoir.

This specimen had a steep tiled roof with little spires at the corners, one surmounted by a ridiculous orna-mental weather-vane. Two round mansard windows were wreathed in stone curlicues. Of the other four front windows, the two on the ground floor were hidden behind closed shutters, but those on the first floor were unshuttered and adorned with elaborately draped net curtains.

The front door was of oak, surmounted by a med-allion and accoutred with various brass fittings: a peep-hole, a letter-box and an old-fashioned knocker.

On one side of this modest residence rose a new six-storey apartment block, and on the other a small private house with a carved stone dog peering forlornly up the avenue de Wagram. The effect was not cheerful.

And Mme Désiris's place wasn't any better. I wouldn't have wanted to live there myself – it made you depressed just to look at it. Perhaps this was because it didn't have a front garden. They cheer a building up no end. But people who live in the XVIIth arrondissement prefer to have their gardens at the back. Selfish devils . . . Still, I had to take my clients, and their favourite architecture, as they came.

I went up to the front door, and had already lifted the knocker when I spotted a more modern alternative. But after I'd rung the bell, I realized the door was ajar. I instinctively gave it a push, and it started to swing silently open. But after about a foot, it stopped. It didn't seem to be on a chain. Whatever was stopping it was lower down, at ground level. Probably one of those 'sausage' draught-excluders. I bent down and groped around a bit. But what my fingers encountered was no sausage: it was round and covered in fabric. In fact, it felt remarkably like a girl's bosom. A bosom no longer heaving, and not all that warm.

The day was getting off to a good start.

I straightened up, my throat so dry it would have taken ten martinis to cure it, and looked around. The street was quiet and deserted. No one had seen me except an inquisitive housemaid over the road who'd been watching my antics through the window. I smiled at her as best I could. Just someone else going about his business, my dear, keeping the capital clean. The dustmen have been. Now it's Nestor's turn. Nestor Burma out prospecting for the undertaker. Cold meat for breakfast as usual.

The girl vanished as if she'd read my mind, and I turned my attention to more serious matters. Having come this far I might as well see the thing through. I leaned against the door hard enough to push it open a bit further, slipped inside and closed it behind me.

There still hadn't been any reaction to the sound of the bell. The house was completely silent except for a clock ticking heavily near by. And the thumping of my heart.

It was dark, too.

I felt around for a light-switch. A wrought-iron lantern with a multicoloured glass shade cast a dull light down on the face of the woman lying inert on the floor. It didn't make her cheeks look any rosier.

I suddenly felt very alone. The hallway contained only a grandfather clock shaped like a coffin, a coat rack with a mirror, a funereal umbrella stand, and the body.

I stood still for a moment, listening for a sign of some presence, human or otherwise. But there was nothing. Then came the throb of an engine, distant at first, then swelling as a car drove up the street, approached, stopped. A door slammed. I tensed. Caught a glimpse of myself in the mirror. White as a ghost. But it turned out to be a false alarm. Whoever it was wasn't coming here.

I pulled myself together and bent over the body.

It was a girl of about twenty, apparently a maid, just up from the country. Rather simple-looking, but quite pretty; her blue nylon overall had ridden up to reveal a pair of legs with which you wouldn't at all mind going for a walk. But her eyes were closed and her nostrils pinched. I was glad, however, to detect a slight breath issuing from her bloodless lips. I sighed with relief: I wasn't a complete vampire after all. I felt her all over but couldn't find any sign of injury. She must have had some sort of shock and passed out. She'd tell me all about it when she came round. But she didn't seem in any hurry to do so. I was obviously going to have to help her, and I set off to find the wherewithal.

A flight of stairs led up from the hall to a landing, where I opened the first door I came to. Inside the room, the shutters were closed, so I turned on the light, revealing a drawing-room about as inviting as a morgue. But it had a sofa.

So I went back downstairs and collected the girl – I don't know what they fed her on but she didn't weigh much. I carried her up and laid her on the sofa, then tried to bring her round, slapping her face and dousing her with cold water from the tap in the kitchen. But without result. She'd passed out in a big way. I decided to let nature take its course, and went to have a look round.

The room opposite was obviously an office. Typewriter, telephone, shelves, filing cabinets and so on. But not a living soul.

I went up to the first floor and stuck my head into what seemed to be a bedroom. A curious smell assailed my nostrils. This must be one of the unshuttered rooms with net draperies that I'd seen from the street. But now I found there were thick velvet curtains inside the net ones, and they were keeping out the light. I went over and drew them back. The April day, with its promise of spring and renewal, burst in so brightly I had to blink. But of the three of us in the room, I was the only one who did.

Ladies first. It seemed to be my lucky day as far as the female form was concerned. She was young, and wearing a very flimsy nightdress. The bedclothes were disordered, with sheets and blankets trailing on to the floor. Her pillow had been thrown on to the bedside table, knocking a lamp over and breaking the bulb.

Mme Désiris – for she it must be – was an unattractive brunette. Her face, now distorted with pain and fear as she lay there on her back, couldn't have been much to look at even under ideal conditions. Fancy getting carried away by her name! I was reminded of a similar experience with Mme Des Oeillets, a lady at the court of Louis XIV who was involved in the Affaire des Poisons. Her name, redolent of the scent of carnations, had always made me imagine someone as enchanting as Mme de Montespan. But then I discovered from reliable historians that she was appallingly plain. Apparently she didn't smell too good either. Anyway, Mme Désiris too was far from palatable, especially with one bullet through her neck and two more through her chest.

The bloke was approaching fifty, but he'd have trouble getting there now. He was dressed in a well-cut grey suit with an impeccable crease in the trousers, highly polished shoes, and a tie only fractionally askew. He'd wanted to bow out in style. He was lying on the far side of the bed, on a rug between it and the window. He'd been shot through the mouth. The bullet had only made a mess coming out. He must have done it himself. A .22 rifle lay near by.

I fought down nausea, slipped on a pair of gloves, and crouched down beside the body. Little did I realize, seeing him stretched out so peacefully, that he'd have such a tale to tell.

I found a wallet in his inside pocket and examined the contents. A small amount of money, some papers of no particular significance, and an identity card in the name of Charles Désiris, engineer. I put it back and explored a small chest of drawers. Nothing of interest.

There was another bedroom next door, which appeared to belong to a man. The bedclothes on the narrow single bed were dishevelled here too. It looked as if someone had stretched out there last night, but hadn't slept much. A sheet of blue writing paper lay on the pillow. Taking care not to touch it, I read what was written on it:

You asked for it.

It was signed *Charles Désiris*.

Digging through the drawers of a desk, I found some official documents from which I learned that Désiris had been born in 1912 (he looked older); that his parents were both dead; and that he and Mlle Jeanne Hélène Labouchère, born in Versailles in 1934 (she looked older than she was, too) had been married by the mayor of the XVIIth arrondissement on 7 July 1954. I made a rapid calculation. Désiris had been forty-two at the time, and the girl only twenty. A daughter had been born just three months after the ceremony, but had lived only ten days. Strange! Usually, if you tangle with kids as young as that you take precautions. Unless . . . But I could ruminate on all that later. I ought to have called the cops a quarter of an hour ago. But then again, I thought, what's a few minutes here or there? I went on with my search.

The only other thing of note that I came up with was a photograph of the man. I reckoned he'd cleared the place out before committing suicide. I studied the portrait, and was struck at once by the broad brow. But most impressive of all was the look in his eye: it reflected an inner flame, a longing for something out of reach, a thirst for the absolute. It was the look of a genius, or a madman. It's easy to be wise after the event, but I was tempted to say his fateful end was written in his face.

Just as I was putting the photograph and the documents back in the desk, a cry rang out below, and I rushed downstairs to find the maid back in the land of the living. She was standing with a dazed expression in the doorway of the room I'd left her in, and I could see it wouldn't take much to make her pass out again. I gave her a paternal pat on the shoulder, but instead of being reassured she just stared back at me with her mouth wide open.

'No need to be frightened,' I said soothingly. 'I'm from the police.'

'Police?' she said blankly.

'Yes. I expect you were going to call us anyway, after you found . . .'

She shuddered.

'Have you . . . have you seen . . . ?' she stammered.

'Yes,' I said. 'But let's not talk about it for the moment. You've got to get your strength back first. Isn't there anything to drink around here?'

She didn't answer, so I took her by the arm and led her into the kitchen, where I unearthed a bottle of a useful-looking brew and poured out a generous measure for her and another for myself. After a second round she began to look better.

'What's your name?' I asked.

'Marie Perrichaux,' she said. 'But Madame called me Mariette.'

'Well, Mariette,' I said, 'my name's Nestor Burma. I expect that rings a bell.'

It did.

'I overheard Madame asking to speak to you on the telephone yesterday,' she said. 'I couldn't help it.'

'I understand. Do you know why she wanted to see me?'

'Didn't she say?'

'No. She just made an appointment. Do you know why?'

'No.'

Poor Mme Désiris. I could still hear her now: 'Hello. I'd like to speak to M. Nestor Burma please . . . Oh! It's you. How do you do, monsieur? Mme Jeanne Désiris speaking . . . I believe you undertake work of a confidential kind . . . There's something I'd like you to do for me . . . Could you, for instance, trace the source of a sudden increase in someone's income? . . . You could! I'm so glad . . . Could you come to my house tomorrow morning at nine?'

I don't remember her exact words, but that was the gist of it. Sudden increase in income, indeed! She'd just said the first thing that came into her head. People are so complicated! Why couldn't she just say: 'I'm worried about my husband. Could you find out what he's up to?'

Anyhow, all that was immaterial now.

But I went on quizzing the maid.

'How did they get on together?'

'So-so.'

'Not too well?'

'So-so.'

'Have you been working here long?'

'Six months.'

'And before that?'

'I lived with my parents.' She made a vague gesture towards the south.

'So this was your first job?' I said.

'Yes.'

Too bad. I lit my pipe.

'They slept in separate rooms, didn't they?'

'Yes.'

'They weren't at all close, then?'

Suddenly she turned pale again and clutched her forehead.

'Ooh,' she groaned, 'I do feel awful.'

'Not surprising, after a shock like that.'

'I wasn't feeling well before I – before I saw—'

'Never mind just yet about what you saw. What do you mean, you weren't feeling well before?'

'I overslept, and got up late with a splitting headache. I didn't even hear the alarm go off!'

'Nor the shots?'

'Nothing.'

'How did you feel when you went to bed last night?' I asked.

'I was terribly sleepy.'

'Do you usually have a drink last thing? Some hot milk, perhaps?'

'No,' she said indignantly. 'What do you take me for? An old woman?'

'And with your dinner?'

'A glass of wine, like everyone else.'

'Do you have your own special bottle?'

'Yes.'

'Good,' I said, refilling her glass. 'Here . . .'

I held it out to her. 'Have a drop more. This lot isn't drugged.'

'Drugged?' she said. 'What do you mean?'

'I mean your wine last night *was*. Your boss had things to do, and he didn't want to be disturbed.'

'Well, I never!' she gasped.

She couldn't get over it even with the help of the Scotch, though it helped.

'Is there any wine left in your bottle?'

'I think so, yes.'

'Well, the cops will analyse it and confirm what I say . . . Talking of them, how did you come to discover the tragedy? I know it's painful, but I'm going to have to call the police shortly and they'll ask you even more questions. So a little rehearsal won't do any harm.'

She shrugged.

'There's not much to tell. I got up late, as I said, not feeling very well, had a bit of a wash and started to get dressed. Then I saw how late it was and just put an overall on over my slip.'

At this point she realized her overall was yawning wide open, a pleasure to behold. She blushed and pulled it to.

'As I went downstairs I knocked at Madame's door for some reason or other. As she didn't answer, I opened the door and saw them. First Madame, then I went in a bit further and saw Monsieur.'

'Just a minute,' I said. '*How* did you see them? Was the light already on?'

'No. I switched it on as I went in.'

She frowned. Something was troubling her.

'Strange, isn't it?'

'What is?' I said.

'The little things you do automatically when something really serious is happening. And they're the things you remember . . . I couldn't for the life of me tell you what I did after seeing the . . . well, afterwards. I don't even know how I got out of the room! But I do know I took the trouble to turn off the light. Stupid, isn't it?'

'Quite natural,' I said. 'Nothing to be ashamed of. Happens all the time. So, the lights were off when you went in. Since your boss couldn't have carried out his plan in the dark, he must have turned on the bedside light, and then it got knocked down and smashed. He didn't need any light, afterwards, to put a bullet in himself. You switched on when you came in, and off again when you went out. There! That's how it was, then . . . I know the coppers – always looking for little inconsistencies. They'd have spent hours pestering you about it. If we explain what happened we'll save them a lot of work. Let's hope they're grateful.'

'What do you think they'll do to me?' she asked anxiously. 'Am I going to be in trouble?'

'No reason you should be,' I said. 'What you saw gave you a shock, and you just ran out.'

'I suppose so. But don't ask me what I did once I got out on to the landing. I don't remember anything. All I know is I woke up down on the drawing-room sofa.'

'I'd put you there.'

I explained how I'd found the front door ajar, with her lying unconscious just inside.

'Your one idea must have been to run for help, but no sooner did you unbolt and unlock the front door than your strength failed and you fainted. Flat out.'

She didn't say anything for a moment. Then she ran her hand across her forehead.

'Yes,' she said. 'That must have been what happened.'

'What did your boss do for a living?' I asked.

'He was an engineer, I think. He used to leave the house early in the morning, before eight o'clock, and he didn't get back until quite late in the evening. After midnight sometimes. Sometimes he didn't come back at all.'

'How did he treat you?'

'He said good morning and good night, that's all. He wasn't very talkative.'

'And what about Madame?' I said. 'Did she have a job or anything?'

'No. She used to just sit around. Not very cheerful.'

I looked at my watch. Time to tell the cops. I made my way to the telephone in the office, Mariette at my heels. With two stiffs in the house, she wasn't going to stay on her own. Before I picked up the phone I glanced through a few drawers. But Désiris had cleared out here even more thoroughly than in his bedroom. He hadn't left anything behind him. That was the only disconcerting element in this commonplace affair. I dialled the CID, and soon heard the gravelly tones of Superintendent Florimond Faroux.

'Hello,' I said. 'Nestor Burma here.'

He smelled a rat straight away.

'What's the damage?'

'One bedside lamp kaput,' I said.

'Are you pulling my leg?' he growled.

'No,' I said, 'it's the truth. If you want more detail you'll have to get over here.'

'Where's here?'

'Rue Alphonse-de-Neuville.' I gave him the number. 'I could have phoned the local super, but I prefer dealing with the head man . . .'

'Cut it out,' he said. 'What's this all about?'

'It looks like either a death pact or a murder followed by a suicide. You know more about such fine distinctions than I do.'

He hung up without saying whether he was coming or not. But if I knew him, he was already leaping into a car in the courtyard of 36, quai des Orfèvres, thinking to himself: 'A death pact! Discovered by Nestor Burma? A likely story!'

I hung up too, and went to open the front door so that Faroux and his men could rush in without let or hindrance. Then I took Mariette back to the kitchen and got her to show me the famous bottle of wine.

And it was there that the law found us, standing next to the third dead'un: the whisky bottle.

There were so many of them you'd have thought they'd come to raise a siege. Florimond had brought along not only his own Grégoire and Fabre, both cops of my acquaintance, but also a gaggle of others from the local station.

'Right, Burma,' said Faroux at once, 'you can start by telling me what you've touched. It'll save time.'

'Only the maid,' I said, pointing to Mariette. She was leaning against the table, terrified. The cops looked so fierce they'd have frightened a tax inspector.

'That'll do!' snapped Faroux. 'Where are the corpses?'

'Upstairs.'

'Come on, lads,' he said to his flock.

Then to me, noticing I was about to tag along: 'You stay here with the maid. If we need you we'll let you know.'

He left one constable to keep an eye on us, and went upstairs.

We sat down and waited in silence, I smoking my pipe and Mariette lost in thought. Her overall was still yawning at the bosom. As if anyone could yawn at a bosom like that. Her legs weren't exactly concealed either. The young copper was busy giving her the once and twice and three times over.

At least an hour went by while Faroux and his gang tramped back and forth, crashing up and down the stairs, making telephone calls, letting in the coroner, admitting the photographer, going through all the usual rigmarole.

Finally, as Mariette was getting jumpy again with all that waiting about, Fabre came in and signed her to follow him. They went out, leaving me alone with the copper.

Shortly afterwards Faroux came in and took a seat.

'I don't know why you bothered me,' he grumbled. 'It's obviously either a double suicide or a murder followed by a suicide. The local man could easily have dealt with it.'

'But he doesn't know me,' I said.

'Quite,' he said. 'How come you were here?'

'I had an appointment with the dead woman,' I said.

'What about?'

'I don't know. She called me yesterday afternoon and asked me to come here at nine-thirty this morning. She didn't say what it was all about.'

Faroux didn't need to know exactly when I'd arrived. He'd only make a fuss, and tell me I shouldn't have waited so long before letting him know.

'And you haven't any idea?' he said.

'Yes, I have,' I said, 'now I've seen the butchery that went on up there. The man didn't do that on the spur of the moment. Maybe he'd been behaving strangely lately, and she was worried. Maybe he'd threatened her, and she was looking for protection. For some reason or other she didn't want to complain to the regular police, so she came to a private detective. But it was too late . . . Anyway, I don't see how I could have saved her from her fate.'

Faroux shrugged. 'Well, let's not make heavy weather of it,' he said. 'He killed her, then he killed himself. They'll be buried side by side and the file will be closed. But we have to go through the usual routine just the same. Fabre and Grégoire are taking care of the maid, upstairs. We'll see if what she says ties in with your version. What *is* your version? Don't worry, it's only routine.'

I told him the whole story, then produced the bottle of wine that had probably been drugged. He got up without a word, took hold of it carefully, and disappeared.

Shortly afterwards there was a commotion on the stairs. The law had all the information it wanted and was getting ready to pull out. My policeman and I joined the rest in the hall, where Faroux was giving his final instructions about who was to stay and who was to go.

I noticed Mariette standing next to Inspector Fabre. She'd put a few clothes on since I saw her last, and made up her face a bit, and she looked quite something in her little grey suit and red overcoat. She didn't look at all like a goose girl any more, despite her company.

I smiled at her and she smiled back, though rather feebly.

'They're taking me away,' she said anxiously.

'We have to get her statement,' said Fabre.

'Don't fret,' I said to her. 'When these chaps get the chance to spend a few hours with a pretty girl, they make the most of it. It's a change from the unshaven blokes they usually have to deal with. Not to mention their own wives.'

'Talking of unshaven blokes,' said Faroux to me with a laugh, 'you can come along too.'

2 Some clues about the body

The next day at about ten I was just telling myself this case wasn't going to ensure me a regular income in my old age when the phone rang. It was my chum Marc Covet, the journalist and soak on the *Crépuscule*. I was surprised he hadn't called me before. He explained why.

'I've just got back from Marseilles,' he said. 'I was there to do a piece on the Sarfotti gang. And now I'm back I find all this fuss about the Désiris case. How come you're mixed up in it? According to the cops your discovery of the bodies was a complete coincidence. You happened to be going down the street when you spotted the maid's hand through a crack in the front door. And so on.'

The day before, in his office, Faroux and I had agreed not to mention the fact that Mme Désiris had made an appointment with me. As she was dead and no one would ever know the reason for her call, there was no point in complicating matters and stirring up speculation. We could have suppressed my involvement altogether if there hadn't been two or three journalists hanging about when we got to the quai des Orfèvres.

'It isn't true, is it?' Marc went on suspiciously.

'Yes. It is.'

'Are you usually out and about so early?'

'I like to take advantage of the spring.'

'Not today, though.'

'I'm afraid I might find some more corpses.'

'Don't tell me that worries you!'

'I do when it causes trouble and gets me suspected of heaven knows what.'

'Are you a suspect?' he said excitedly.

'Between you and me, yes. Are you going to town on it?'

'Maybe. It depends. It's a good middle-class subject. It might be working up something in the Balzac line. The readers are getting fed up with gangsters. Sarfotti's special, but otherwise hoodlums are out. Balzac would make a nice change.'

'Go on!' I said. 'Your readers couldn't tell the difference between *Eugénie Grandet* and the telephone directory.'

'Then it's a good opportunity to teach them. Listen: the cops are making out they don't know the reasons for the suicide. Are they really in the dark?'

'Yes. But I think the bloke was mad. I saw a photo of him. You could tell he was barmy from his eyes.'

'It's a possibility,' said Marc. 'The chap who replaced me while I was away picked up a few bits of information. It seems Désiris was an inventor, and they're always nuts.'

'What did he invent?'

'I don't know. Maybe he didn't invent anything. But he was working on something.'

'What was that?'

'We don't know yet. But I've sent two people to try to find out.'

'Well, good luck,' I said. 'I've got nothing more to tell you.'

'What about the maid?' he said. 'She's disappeared.'

'Probably gone home to the country.'

In fact I'd asked Hélène, my secretary, to put the girl up for the time being, partly to keep her out of the way of journalists and partly to help her get over the shock. But I wasn't going to tell Marc Covet that.

'Right. Well, thanks a lot, anyway,' he said. 'If anything unexpected comes up . . .'

'Highly unlikely,' I said.

That was the end of the conversation. I then made a call myself, to a friend I knew to be looking for a maid. I told her Mariette hadn't got any references because her last employers hadn't given her any, and that they wouldn't answer the phone . . . They were the Désiris couple that all the papers were talking about.

'Oh, how exciting,' she said. 'Send her round at once!'

I told her to get in touch with Hélène and hung up. That was a good job done.

The telephone rang again straight away.

'Monsieur Nestor Burma?' came a grating voice.

'Yes.'

'This is Monsieur Labouchère.'

'Monsieur—?'

'Madame Désiris's father.'

'Oh, I see . . . Yes?'

'I'd like to meet you and ask you a few questions.'

'Right. When?'

'The sooner the better,' he said.

He gave me the address of his apartment in the avenue de la Grande Armée.

It was in an imposing edifice constructed around the turn of the century as a private mansion, no expense spared: the balconies were supported by caryatides. And the middle-class respectability of the house extended to its occupants, from the attics right down to the concierge's lodge. Unlike the neighbouring buildings, this one hadn't allowed its ground floor to be invaded by shops selling sports or motor accessories, although it stood on the edge of an area where that was happening more and more.

The concierge told me M. Labouchère lived on the first floor, and the door was opened by a flunkey in a striped waistcoat. His expression reflected the fact that there'd been a death in the family. He was obviously expecting me, and led the way into a drawing-room where a slightly stooped but remarkably fit-looking man of about sixty was waiting for me. His face was bony, his eyes hard behind his glasses, and he was dressed as if he'd just been chairing a board meeting. But on the table he was sitting at were strewn almost all the Paris dailies. He gave me an appraising look and nodded towards a chair. I sat down. The flunkey melted away.

'I asked you to come because I wanted to find out what your role was in all this. From what I've gathered from the papers and the police conducting the investigation, it seems it was you who found the . . . who discovered what had happened. Quite by chance. You were just passing by. A remarkable coincidence.'

He sounded like Marc Covet.

'I don't really know what my role is myself,' I said,

trying not to smile. 'But you're right to be sceptical, monsieur. I didn't find the . . . what you're talking about . . . by chance. Superintendent Faroux and I adopted that story to avoid pointless gossip in the press. But I thought Faroux had told you the truth.'

'Which is that you'd been in contact with my daughter?'

'Yes. I had an appointment with her yesterday morning.'

'In a professional capacity?'

'Yes.'

'Had you been working for her long?'

'Since the previous day. She'd hired me by telephone. Tried to, rather. But I don't know what for. I was going to her house to discuss it.'

He was silent for a moment, thinking. He rubbed his chin with a bony hand. Then he looked at me keenly, sighed, and said in a dull voice: 'It doesn't really matter any more. He killed her and then killed himself. Justice has been done. But I'm interested in anything to do with my daughter, even now that she's dead. And I just wanted to know why she got in touch with you. But as you don't know yourself . . .'

'I suppose she must have felt she needed protection. Her husband may have seemed to be behaving strangely all of a sudden. Dangerously. You knew him – wouldn't you have said he was slightly unstable?'

'I wouldn't say I actually knew him. He came here out of the blue and seduced Jeanne – a man of his age! – and then, when she was pregnant, we had no choice but to agree to the marriage.'

Just as I'd thought when I read those documents the day before.

'And Jeanne loved him, too, the foolish girl!' he went

on with a mirthless laugh. 'No, he wasn't mad. On the contrary, he was very lucid. He knew what he was doing when he seduced my daughter. He had his eye on my fortune, thought I'd hand him over a part of it straight away. But he was mistaken. He didn't get a penny. I let them have that house of mine in the rue Alphonse-de-Neuville, and left them to fend for themselves. I was furious with both of them, and from then on we didn't really keep in touch. My wife used to see Jeanne from time to time – she used to go and hand over the allowance I finally agreed to give her. It wasn't much – just enough to pay for her clothes and a maid. Nothing for him! He thought he'd made his fortune by marrying Jeanne, but I saw to it that he had to go on working at the Dugat car factory in Levallois!'

He stared into space. He was imagining his son-in-law on the way to the factory first thing in the morning. Seeing him put on his overalls – he might have had quite a senior job, but he was still only a factory hand. A strange situation: married to a wealthy heiress, living in a huge house, and yet being obliged to work not because you wanted to but to make ends meet, just like everybody else.

I looked at Labouchère. He was licking his lips, still gloating over his revenge. I wondered how many times he'd come close to death himself without knowing it; how many times Désiris had felt like killing his father-in-law before he finally did away with himself and his wife. It was to the old man sitting opposite me that the cryptic 'You asked for it' had been addressed. It was a kind of curse.

He emerged from his reverie and noticed I was still there.

'I don't know why I'm telling you all this,' he said.

'Nor do I,' I said. 'Perhaps you need to confide in someone. It's only human.'

'Maybe it's because I like you.'

I didn't answer. I wasn't going to say I was flattered. I didn't give a damn whether he liked me or not. *I* didn't like *him*. Or his son-in-law, or even his daughter, although I couldn't help feeling a bit sorry for her.

Now it was my turn to ponder. I began to think how unlucky Jeanne Labouchère had been. Quite a nice figure, it was true – I'd noticed that the day before. But what an ugly mug! There couldn't have been many other suitors knocking around when Désiris and his ulterior motives came on the scene. The difference in age had only speeded things up. Maybe she'd regretted the marriage later on, when they'd drifted apart. Mariette had said she wasn't very cheerful. So why hadn't they got a divorce? – there weren't any children to consider. From his point of view the answer was obvious. Labouchère, being ten or twelve years older than his son-in-law, would probably snuff it first, and then Désiris stood to come in for part of the inheritance. As far as the wife was concerned, perhaps her upbringing had left her opposed to divorce on principle? On the other hand, it's said that the females of certain species are faithful for life to their first mate. Perhaps some women are the same? Perhaps she still loved Désiris even though their relationship was over.

Now I came back to earth.

'I gather he was an inventor,' I said. Then, echoing Marc Covet: 'They're always a bit odd.'

Labouchère shrugged. 'There was nothing odd about him, and he wasn't an inventor. He was an engineer. Quite a clever one, apparently, though I never went into the matter. He used to complain that some of his ideas had been stolen by his employers. Utter nonsense . . . Anyway, enough about him. All I wanted to know was what your relationship was with my daughter.'

'Well,' I said again, 'I can only suppose she was afraid her husband was going to do something extreme, didn't want to tell her troubles to you or to the police, and came to me instead.'

'Did you infer all that from what she said on the phone?'

'No,' I said. 'From what I saw yesterday morning. There was clearly more to the matter than what she'd suggested on the phone. *That* didn't strike me as very convincing.'

'What did she say?'

'She asked me if I could find out the source of a sudden increase in someone's income.'

He started stroking his chin again.

'H'm,' he said. 'I don't see what she could have meant by that, either. Unless . . . Wait a minute. He wasn't working at Dugat's any more. He left there several months ago. Jeanne said something about it at the time – something about his circumstances having changed. I don't remember the exact date – what he got up to was of no interest to me. I advised her to divorce him, but she wouldn't. So I left her to sort it out – I didn't want to know what went on between them. Anyway, he left Dugat's – ' he grimaced ' – and what happened next I found out from the police, though to save time I pretended I knew already. He bought a workshop on the river, on the Ile de la Grande-Jatte, and set up there on his own. He had two men working for him, though he sacked them both last December, I remember. I wonder what he got up to in that workshop.'

'Putting the finishing touches to some invention, perhaps,' I suggested.

He just grunted, then went on: 'When Jeanne first told me he wasn't at Dugat's any more, I said to myself: "What's he going to live on now? He'll soon be round here trying to touch me." But he didn't come, and now I come to think of it, it must have cost him quite a bit to start up a business of his own like that, and to pay his staff. Not an enormous amount, but still . . . Even if he had some savings . . .'

'Could he have been left some money?'

'No. He didn't have any family.'

In that case the workshop on the Ile de la Grande-Jatte would come to the old man whose money Désiris had been after. Fate can play some funny tricks.

'He must have got hold of some capital somehow,' Labouchère went on. 'Do you think that's what my daughter wanted to see you about?'

'If it had only come in in the last few days, perhaps. But what you're talking about goes back several months . . .'

'Yes, of course. Unless she took all that time to make up her mind. What did she say to you exactly?'

I told him again, which didn't get either of us any farther forward.

We were both silent for a while. There was no more to be said.

I stood up.

'Before you go,' he said, 'I owe you something for expenses. For coming to see me. And for going to see my daughter.'

The days went by.

No more was heard about 'the gruesome affair in the

rue Alphonse-de-Neuville', as the papers had dubbed it. There being no reason for delay, the police soon concluded that Jeanne Désiris had been killed by her husband, who then committed suicide. As simple as that. Of the dead man's two employees, one, an Algerian, had vanished into thin air, swallowed up by the FLN or some similar group of freedom fighters. The other, when traced, had no sensational revelations to offer. His boss had been working on a new kind of engine. Two points had not been cleared up, and probably never would. What was the reason for the tragedy? And why was there just over a million francs left in the dead man's bank account? (Another addition to the father-in-law's money bags!) Was it Désiris's savings? Whatever the explanation, the police didn't waste any time on such trifles. They had other fish to fry.

The dismembered body of a woman had been found on a piece of wasteland in Châtillon, a Molotov cocktail's throw from the atomic power station. A bank clerk had been killed in a hold-up in the rue Vivienne. There'd been a gangland shoot-out in Montmartre. Then there was the mysterious torture and murder of a woman suspected of being an accomplice of the Sarfotti gang. (These toughs were the subject of Marc's Marseilles assignment. They used to smuggle tobacco from Tangiers to the south coast of France in an old submarine.) Then there was the lady of independent means – almost the last of an endangered species – who'd been stabbed to death in Sceaux. (She turned out to be a gentleman of independent means who'd been going about dressed as a woman for the last sixty years.)

In short, spring was going to the underworld's head. Faroux had his work cut out. So did I: two or three cases of married men having a bit on the side; an industrialist who asked me to keep an eye on his accountant . . .

And Désiris?

Not a word on the subject, until one fine evening the front-page headline of the *Crépu* proclaimed:

THE TRUTH BEHIND THE SUICIDE OF CHARLES DESIRIS. TRAGEDY OF AN INVENTOR.

The article was by Marc Covet, and from it I learned that Désiris had invented – or started to invent – a 'revolutionary' motor. The invention had been patented, which was how Covet had dug it out. On closer examination, Désiris's discovery had proved less epoch-making thàn had been supposed. To be accurate, it was incomplete: some of his ideas hadn't been carried through to their logical conclusion. Covet suggested that the reason for this was that the engineer had run out of inspiration.

Thus, he went on, *conscious that his creative powers were declining, Désiris took his own life and that of his young wife. Either he acted with her consent, or, driven mad by the reverses he'd suffered, he avenged his frustrations on his innocent spouse.*

I grabbed the phone and called Covet.

'You seem very interested in Désiris,' I said.

'Your fault,' he retorted. 'I wouldn't have kept on at the story if you hadn't been mixed up in it.'

'I wasn't.'

'So you said, but I didn't have to believe you. It turned out I was wrong there, but just the same I was able to scratch together a pretty good article, don't you think? – *and* provide a plausible explanation for the suicide.'

'Did you invent the bit about the invention, or is it true?' I said.

'A bit of both.'

'What do you mean?'

'It's true Désiris had done the groundwork for what might have been a new motor. The experts say his basic ideas were sound, but he was no good at applying them. He'd dried up. And as a story about a genius whose mind fails him is more spectacular than one about a mere case of fraud, that's what I chose to write about. As I said before, our readers always like something new.'

'Fraud?' I said.

'Yes. Désiris must have been a bit of a crook. When his research got stuck, he tried to get money – and not peanuts, either – out of various people. But naturally he'd never go into detail, so the negotiations almost always came to nothing. The money they found in his bank account must have come from some prize sucker – who thought he'd better keep quiet about it afterwards. A bit of a card, old Désiris.'

'I agree,' I said. 'But all this doesn't explain his suicide.'

'Doesn't it? His creative powers were failing, and he was afraid his swindling activities would come to light. He lost his head.'

'Perhaps,' I said. 'Anyhow . . .'

'Yes . . . He's dead, anyhow. So what's the difference?'

A few more days went by, during which I half-expected

a call from old Labouchère. I thought the *Crépu* article might make him pick up the phone. But no. Days became weeks. Whether he'd been an inventor or just a hoaxer, Désiris was obviously going to be forgotten, along with the dismembered woman, her still unidentified killer, and all the rest. The summer holidays came along, followed by the usual period of convalescence.

Then November came nosing through the misty air.

3 Double trouble

The girl had arranged herself on the couch in a position designed to show her charms to advantage. One leg was folded up underneath her, the other trailing, and all she had on, apart from her stiletto-heeled shoes, was a pair of black stockings drawn up tight by a flimsy black nylon suspender belt. Above an ample and arrogant bosom, a cascade of glossy hair framed a cute little face in which disingenuousness and depravity were inextricably mingled.

But it was only a photograph – one of thirty or more of a similar kind in *Purely Parisian Thrills*, an under-the-counter girlie magazine.

Tearing my eyes away from its pages, I looked at the silent young woman sitting in an armchair a few yards away from me. We were in a large and luxurious drawing-room looking out on one of the upper corners of the Arc de Triomphe. Her legs – I'm talking about the real woman now – were just as enticing in their silvery stockings as those of the girl in the photo. Since my hostess, the blonde film star Dany Darnys, was unfortunately fully clothed, I couldn't tell if her bosom too stood up to the comparison. From what I could see it was less voluminous. But it would do very well. As for her face, it was oozing with oomph.

'Well?' she said.

She'd called me earlier and asked me to come and see her. And the moment I walked through the door she'd thrust the magazine at me, saying indignantly: 'Look at pages ten, eleven and twelve and tell me what you think of those pictures!'

Only then had she offered me a seat and a Scotch, and told me I could smoke my pipe. Then she'd sat down herself, leaving me to revel in the festival of flesh. Finally I reached a verdict.

'Most people would swear it was you,' I said.

'But it's not!'

'I know that,' I said. 'I wasn't born yesterday. But the publishers of this rag have been lucky for once. Up till now the imitations they've tried to put across of Brigitte Bardot and Sophia Loren have been very feeble. But in your case it's different. They've found a perfect double.'

She blinked.

'Do you mean to say Bardot and Loren have been featured in this thing too?'

'Some issues have been devoted almost entirely to them.'

'You seem to know a lot about it,' she said curtly. 'You don't read this horror, do you?'

I smiled.

' "Read" isn't exactly the word,' I said, secretly amused at this display of prudishness. 'Anyhow, I know which I'd choose if I had to decide between a genuine profile of a politician and a fake view of Bardot's back-side. Or of yours either, for that matter.'

This quip got an icy reception. She stubbed out her cigarette impatiently, and it joined several others in a crystal ashtray on the glass coffee-table. Between the ashtray and the whisky decanter I noticed a kind of leather pouch.

'There's no accounting for tastes,' she said. 'To get back to these photographs, I think they must be illegal.'

'Are you going to sue?'

'No,' she said. 'There's been enough scandal already.'

'Not to mention that you'd probably lose the case.'

'Lose the case? Why?'

'Well, I'm not a lawyer,' I said, 'but I've had a lot of experience and I've got a good memory. The publishers must know what they're doing, and how far they can go without putting themselves in the wrong. It's a similar sort of racket to the one that certain high-class brothels used to operate. They'd hunt out girls who looked like famous courtesans or actresses, and so on, and palm them off on clients as the originals. The Guy Sisters were the attraction at one time, I remember.'

She was shocked. Apparently she thought the Guy Sisters were nuns. She seemed reassured when I told her they were a couple of dancers who performed in the altogether at the Café de Paris around 1925.

'I don't remember that anyone ever sued then,' I went on. 'The thing is, you can't stop someone from looking like someone else, even if that someone else is a public figure. Nor can you stop people from having themselves photographed in whatever get-up or situation they choose (you'll notice that the pictures in *Purely Parisian Thrills* deliberately stop short of actual pornography!). So, as there's no law, either, against using make-up, lighting and camera angles to accentuate the likeness between a "double" and the original, I don't think you've got a case. The publishers of *Thrills* may not win any prizes for ethics, but I don't think their activities can be considered criminal. And, as the clients of the brothels I mentioned no doubt concluded, a lawsuit would only make sure that what was known only to a few would be broadcast to everybody.'

'It's a pleasure to hear you talk, Monsieur Burma,' said Dany Darnys with a wry smile. 'The things you know! There are no flies on you, as my script-writers would have me say.'

I tried to look modest.

'So I've no redress against these people?'

'I don't think so. Not legally. They can say it's only a joke.'

She lit another Gitane.

'Some joke! . . . Couldn't they just use models who don't resemble anyone else?'

'They do sometimes,' I said. 'But if the girls look like celebrities it adds a bit of spice.'

'Well, it's beyond me,' she sighed, 'but thanks for explaining the position. The upshot is, I can't take them to court – not that I intended to, anyway. But I do mean to stop them. And that's why I sent for you.'

'What do you want me to do?'

'Nothing difficult,' she said. 'I could do it myself, but I'd rather it was you.'

She threw away her cigarette and lit yet another.

'I want you to contact this girl and bring her to see me. I have a proposition to make to her.'

'What sort of proposition, if you don't mind my asking?'

She blushed slightly.

'A perfectly honourable one! I'll get her another job . . . Whatever she fancies. Perhaps I could even take her on as my stand-in . . . Anyhow, I'll find something, but I want her to stop what she's doing now.'

It was an ingenious enough solution. I said as much.

'I'm glad you approve. Does that mean I can count on your help?'

'Certainly.'

She leaned forward and picked up the leather pouch. It turned out to contain a cheque book and an elegant gold fountain-pen. As her slender, rosy-tipped fingers were poised to write: 'About your fee,' she said. 'I don't know what the going rate is. How about . . . ?' She suggested a sum that proved how ardently she longed to meet her double. Money was obviously no object.

'That'll be fine,' I said.

She filled in the cheque and held it out. I got up to take it, still holding *Purely Parisian Thrills* in my other hand. It was a brand-new copy with a crease down the middle.

'By the way, how did this come into your possession?' I asked.

'It arrived through the post three days ago.'

'Just as I thought,' I said. 'By letter post in a sealed envelope?'

'Yes,' she said. 'Very discreet.'

'Any idea who might have sent it?'

'Oh, it must have been one of my professional friends, wanting to give me a pleasant surprise. You know what actors are like.'

Or maybe it was from the publisher, I thought; a prelude to some serious negotiations.

'Right, I must be off,' I said. 'As soon as I've got the girl's name and address I'll let you know. But don't expect to hear from me for a few days.'

'Take all the time you need,' she said. 'I have confidence in you. They say you're very smart.'

'Really? Who are "they"?'

'Marcel Viénot, the man who advised me to contact you. Perhaps you know him.'

'No,' I said. 'Is he a friend of yours?'

'Yes,' she said.

'One of the kind you mentioned just now?'

'Oh, no! Marcel's not an actor. He's in the motor-car industry. He's a real friend, not a competitor.'

'Talking of which,' I said, 'can you really think of any of your competitors, male or female, who are likely to have sent you a thing like this?'

'I can think of two, for a start . . .'

She gave me their names.

'Well, mademoiselle,' I said, 'I think that's about all. I'll just take the address of the magazine and then I really will be going.'

'Take the wretched thing with you,' she said, 'if you think it can be of any use.'

It might. If ever I felt lonely. I put it in my pocket. She rose, smoothed her skirt down over her slim thighs, and led the way to the front door. As I retrieved my coat, she struggled with bolts and chain and so on.

'I'm as brave as the next person,' she explained, 'but ever since I was attacked . . .'

'What?'

'Don't you read the papers? They talked of nothing else. It happened about a month ago, just before my films came out . . .'

Films with an 's'. Her first two films, which had come out together and made her famous overnight.

'Two men must have followed me,' she went on.

'One per film,' I thought, laughing to myself. But I said politely: 'Oh yes, I remember now.'

Dany Darnys and her 'Mysterious Attackers'! That was a good one! Everyone had twigged at once that it was a rather feeble publicity stunt. But wait a minute! Supposing it had been real! Supposing she *had* been attacked, but had been taken for someone else? For the model from *P.P.T.*, for instance!

'Go on,' I said.

'Ever since, I've been . . . what did my psycho-analyst friend call it? . . . oh yes, I've been traumatized . . . I feel I must barricade myself in. I have the feeling that anyone who does more than glance at me means me some harm. And I can't stand the sight of irises.'

'Oh really,' I said. 'Why's that?'

'Because the two men who attacked me kept referring to them. Iris this and iris that. They must have been mad.'

I gave a start.

Iris. Désiris. I couldn't have stumbled on the body again, could I?

Stop fantasizing, Burma, I told myself sternly, borrowing another phrase from the psychoanalysts.

'Let's go back inside,' I said. 'I've got a few more questions to ask you.'

She looked surprised, but did as I asked.

'I want you to be frank with me,' I began. 'Was that incident with the two men just a publicity stunt, as everyone thought, or did it really happen?'

'Oh, I know what people thought,' she said with a sigh. 'But it happened all right.'

There was an unmistakable ring of sincerity in her voice.

'I believe you,' I said. 'Tell me about it.'

'Well . . . I'd just got home. I was on my own – it was the maid's day off. The door-bell rang. So I went to answer it . . . and these two men grabbed hold of me and dragged me in here.'

'What did they look like?'

'Just ordinary.'

'If my memory serves me right,' I said, 'you weren't able to give any details about them. You just said they were nasty-looking types. As a matter of fact, that was one reason people didn't believe your story. After all, you'd just finished making a couple of detective films!'

'I was too upset to notice anything. But I'm sure there *wasn't* anything unusual about them.'

'Go on.'

'What else can I tell you? They made all kinds of threats, and talked a lot of nonsense, especially about irises and camouflage. That's what made me think they were crazy.'

'What sort of threats?'

'I don't know,' she said. ' "Don't pretend you don't know what we're talking about! We'll do this, that or the other to you if you play the fool!" They were trying to intimidate me – as if I wasn't paralysed with fright already!'

' "Iris . . ." ' I said. 'Look, it couldn't have been "Désiris", could it?'

'Perhaps,' she said. 'But why . . . ?'

But I waved her to silence and asked her how the incident ended.

'Quite unexpectedly, thank goodness,' she said. 'They suddenly started swearing, let me go, and left.'

'They'd been actually holding you, had they?'

She reddened.

'Yes,' she said.

'Why are you blushing?'

'No reason.'

'I'll ask you again,' I said. 'Was it a hoax or not?'

'No! . . . Don't you believe I'm telling you the truth?'

'Not the whole truth.'

'But I am!' she cried. 'Anyway, what's it got to do with you? It's all over and done with, and I didn't hire you to stir it all up again! I hired you to—'

'I know,' I said. 'To stop your double from posing in cheap photos for a cheap magazine. But if you were telling me the whole truth you wouldn't be blushing like that. Either you're hiding something, or the whole thing's a pure fabrication.'

'So what? What's it to you?'

'Frankly, nothing. I'm just curious by nature.'

'All right!' she exploded. 'They were trying to rape me! Now are you satisfied? Do you want all the details? They pulled my skirt up over my head, and then . . . well, they didn't get any further. That's when one of them started to swear like a trooper and they ran away. And now *you* can clear out too! If you ask any more questions I'll take my cheque back and get some other detective to find the girl!'

'Now, now,' I said. 'Calm down. I apologize. I didn't mean to upset you or bring back painful memories. It was probably the word "iris" that got me all worked up. You see, Désiris is the name of someone I know, or rather knew. He killed his wife a few months ago, at the beginning of March, and then committed suicide. They didn't live far from you. At the other end of the avenue de Wagram, to be precise.'

'How horrible!' she said. 'Yes, I must have read about it in the papers. Do you think there's some connection, then?'

My head was swimming.

'I don't know,' I said. 'I really don't know . . . My apologies again, mademoiselle.'

'It's all right,' she said with a smile. 'I'm not really angry with you. On the contrary – if anyone casts doubt on the story of the attack again, you'll be able to vouch for me.'

'Yes. So I will!'

I ventured one more question. 'I don't think you ever mentioned the business of the flowers, or the attempted rape, did you?'

'No. I realized no one believed a word I said. They all thought it was just a put-up job, to make people talk about me. So there was no point in going into embarrassing details, was there?'

'Certainly not,' I said. 'And once again, I do apologize.'

We shook hands and I left.

I'd parked my car a bit further down the avenue de Wagram, and after I'd settled down again in the driving seat I opened *Purely Parisian Thrills* to see wnere its publishers hung out. But the only address I could find was a box number for correspondence: Box No. 12 at Post Office No. 90 in the IXth arrondissement. Rather what I'd expected. I also learned that the magazine was printed by a 'special printer', address not supplied. That was no surprise, either. Even the manager seemed to operate under an assumed name. 'Dupont.' If that wasn't a joke it was the next best thing.

I fished a Paris guide out of the glove compartment. Post Office No. 90 was up in the rue Duperré, almost at the corner of the rue Fontaine. I decided to go and give it the once over.

Having seen where the poste restante boxes were, I studied the local collection and delivery times, then phoned Roger Zavatter, the most presentable of my assistants, to tell him I had a little job for him.

'Fire away,' he said.

'She's a blonde,' I said. 'Dany Darnys. Lives in the avenue de Wagram.'

'The one that's just become a star?'

'Yes.'

'What do you want me to do to her?'

'She became a client of ours about half an hour ago, but I want to know more about her. So ferret out what information you can . . . see what she does with her time, day and night. Her contacts, too – especially someone called Marcel Viénot. He knows me but I don't know him.'

'There are plenty of those!'

'He may be linked to the Désiris suicide. Désiris worked in the car business, and so does he.'

I went back to the agency conscious I was poking my nose into something that didn't really concern me. But it wouldn't be the first time. At my office, I got a plain visiting card with just my name on it and added a few words. It now read: 'NESTOR BURMA presents his compliments to the Editor of *P.P.T.*, and informs him that he will shortly be calling on him to discuss a confidential matter.'

I put the card into a brightly coloured envelope that

was bound to attract attention, and addressed and stamped it. Then, as I still had some time to kill before the next stage of Operation *P.P.T.*, I had a little talk with Hélène, my secretary, about the magazine, and about Dany Darnys.

Meanwhile the post office in the rue Duperré would have closed, so I went back there and dropped my brief missive into the outside letter-box.

I must have been the only person in Paris to waste a stamp on having a letter delivered over such a short distance. It was only two or three yards from the general letter-box to Poste Restante Box No. 12.

No wonder I'm always broke.

4 *Régine*

Next morning I posted myself at the post office.

It was eight sharp. Opening time. I bought a stamp to justify my being there, and after having a squint at the poste restante and spotting my red envelope through the glass panel in the front of Box No. 12, went to a corner where no one would notice me, and started reading the papers. As I read I kept an eye on the people coming in and out.

At about ten I saw a conceited-looking young fellow saunter over to Box No. 12. As he opened it, my red envelope fluttered to the floor. He picked it up, studied it for a while (you don't often see them that colour), sniffed at it, then stuffed it, together with the rest of the letters he'd just collected, into his leather brief-case.

I was outside and behind the wheel of my car in a flash. In time to see him come out and get into a rather scruffy little banger parked in the area reserved for post-office vehicles.

When he drove off I followed him to the boulevard Berthier, where he disappeared, brief-case and all, into a neglected-looking house where the upper half of the frontage consisted almost entirely of windows. It looked like one of those former artists' studios that have been converted for photography. I waited for a bit, in case this wasn't his final destination, though I was pretty sure these must be *P.P.T.*'s headquarters. Then I went over to the house and rang the bell. The door opened a crack. Through the chink I could see the astonished face of the man from the post office. *P.P.T.* couldn't have had many visitors. I didn't give him time to ask questions. I just gave the door a good shove and I was in.

'Hey, you!' he yelled, trying to catch hold of me. But I pushed him aside.

'Monsieur Dupont's expecting me,' I said.

The noise we were making had brought a man to the door of a nearby office. There was something in his hand. My red envelope. Perfect timing! Anyone would think we'd rehearsed it.

'What's all the row about, Henri?' he snarled. He was overweight and none too clean. He didn't have much hair, either, and what he did have was greasy. I didn't dare think about his feet.

'How should I know?' said Henri. 'He forced his way in.'

The fat man glared at me out of protruding eyes.

'What do you want?' he snapped.

'You'll know if you open that,' I said, pointing to the envelope. 'It's from me.'

Henri tried to make himself useful. 'Would you like me to . . . ?' he asked.

'No,' said the other. 'I don't know what he thinks he's doing, bursting in like this, but no doubt he'll explain.'

Henri disappeared, and Dupont, if it was he, turned on his heel and went back into his office. I followed. It was an austere place. A calendar on one wall was the only decoration. Not a single pin-up in sight; not a square inch of bosom. M. Dupont wasn't a consumer of his own product. He tore open the red envelope and read what I'd written on the visiting card.

'So . . . You're the private eye, are you?' he said.

'Yes.'

'Delighted to meet you, old chap.'

To my surprise, the hand he held out was clean, firm and not at all clammy.

'I used to be in the same business,' he went on. 'I worked for Marius in Lyons . . . It's a real pleasure to see you, but couldn't you have come in more quietly? Why all the uproar? . . . But never mind that now. Do take a seat.'

I did so. He went and sat down at his desk.

'Confidential matter, eh?' he grunted, glancing again at my card.

'Yes,' I said, producing my copy of *P.P.T.*, open at the pages Dany Darnys had been so upset about.

'This girl – ' I stuck one of the photographs under his nose ' – I'd like her name, address and telephone number if she's got one.'

'Steady on!' said the fat man. 'What do you take me for?'

'A pimp,' I replied, 'when the price is right.'

'Watch what you say!' he protested. 'Why do you have to be so aggressive?'

'I don't know,' I answered. But I knew perfectly well. It was his ugly mug. 'Perhaps this girl's got me worked up.'

'She's certainly got the equipment,' he said.

At that moment a cry rang out somewhere in the building.

'What's that?' I said.

'One of our models being raped, I expect,' he said with heavy irony. 'It happens all the time. Now, where were we?'

There was a sound of raised voices, then a door slammed shut just overhead. The fat man gave a growl, got up and went out into the corridor. I went after him just in time to see a young woman sliding down the banister from the floor above. All she had on were some patches of soap bubbles and a minute pair of panties. Then I realized her feet were slippery, too, and she hadn't walked down because she was afraid of coming a cropper.

'Oh, there you are, Monsieur Dupont,' she squeaked. 'I've just about had enough of that photographer of yours! I'm getting out of here now, and I want my money!'

'You shut your trap,' the fat man replied. 'Don't try to kid us you're an innocent!'

He made to catch hold of her.

I didn't stop to reflect that the soapsuds would let her slip through his fingers. I just clenched my fist and landed him one right on the nose. It made a satisfying 'plop', and he collapsed beneath the astonished gaze of young Henri, who'd reappeared from nowhere, and of another chap, doubtless the randy photographer, who'd stopped half-way down the stairs.

The fat man got up and gave me a dirty look. Not that he was capable of a clean one. 'Get out of here, all of you,' he growled. 'And as for your confidential information, Burma, you can put it up your—'

'OK,' I said. 'Just the place for it.'

'She smashed up one of my cameras!' said the photographer from his perch on the stairs.

'And she still wants to be paid?' gasped Dupont. 'Get the hell out of here! Get out!'

'I want my clothes first!' squawked the soap nymph. 'I wouldn't take your lousy money now anyway! You can keep it, and stick it—'

'Now, now,' I said. 'Let's not start getting vulgar.'

The cheesecake artist disappeared and came back with an armful of clothes which he threw down the stairs, accompanied by an overnight bag and a string of oaths. The girl bent down, extracted a nylon slip from the heap, and rubbed herself down with it. Then she put on a dress and a fur coat, stuffed the wet slip, her stockings and the rest of her undies into the bag, and after slipping her shoes on, running her fingers through her damp hair and tying on a headscarf, she was ready. We walked out together through a hostile silence. Someone slammed the front door loudly behind us.

We walked a little way, then the girl stopped and looked at me with shining brown eyes. Perhaps she wasn't a beauty, but she had charm. Without any make-up and virtually straight out of the bath, she looked wholesome and attractive. A cold wind was blowing now. It caught the stray locks of fair hair that escaped from beneath her scarf.

'That was really good,' she said.

'What?' I asked.

'The punch. A pleasure to watch.'

'It was the least I could do.'

She laughed. 'Do you often indulge in fisticuffs?'

'No,' I said. 'I always feel like it when I come across

a mug like Dupont's, but I usually restrain myself.
There are so many, I wouldn't have time for anything
else. Today was exceptional.'

'You seem to have a pretty low opinion of the human
race,' she said.

'Pretty low,' I said.

'Perhaps you're right,' she said, shrugging and
moving on. 'At least in the case of men like Dupont
and that photographer.'

'Yes,' I said.

'Girls like me, too, huh?' Her voice became suddenly
aggressive. 'Whores. Go on – say it.'

'All right,' I said, 'if you like – I'm easy. What does
it mean, anyway? I've never thought of "whore" as
having a *pejorative* meeting.'

'You are a funny chap, aren't you?' she said.

'So I'm told,' I said. 'But I don't know what that
means, either.'

'You are funny,' she repeated. Then her voice altered
again. 'You know something? I like you . . . er . . . I
don't know what your name is.'

'Nestor Burma,' I said. 'Don't you think that's
funny, too?'

'No. Why should I? My name's Régine Monteuil. I
like you, Nestor.'

'Call me Nes,' I said. 'It's nicer.'

'Yes.'

'So it was my punch that appealed to you, was it?'

'At first, yes – it really did!' she said. 'You see, I'm
being frank with you. I'm sorry I was cross just now.
It was myself I was angry with.' She sighed. 'I don't
know what came over me, refusing to do what that
photographer wanted. What difference would it have

made, one time more or less? I should have let him have his own way. Now I'll be broke again. But no – he really was too disgusting.'

'There's nothing to regret, Régine,' I said. 'Never regret sticking up for yourself. I don't regret laying one on Dupont, do I, even though it was against my own interest? Now I can whistle for the information I was after. Unless . . . As you two are colleagues . . .'

I pulled *Purely Parisian Thrills* out of my pocket. I'd been careful to retrieve it before I left Dupont's office. 'Perhaps you know this girl?'

'Why do you ask?'

'I'm trying to find her.'

'Why? Do you want to sleep with her?' she said. 'Did you hope Dupont would give you her address?'

'Yes,' I said. 'And her name as well. So do you know her or not? I don't want to sleep with her – I want to find her.'

I hesitated for a moment and then decided to lay my cards on the table. I told her exactly why I was looking for Dany Darnys' double.

'So Dupont's going to lose yet another of his models?' Régine said with a smile.

'Yes.'

'She's a friend of mine. Yolande Mège. We live in the same apartment block in the rue du Dobropol. If you want to go there I can give you a lift.'

Our chat had brought us to a smart little convertible, apparently the property of my new girl-friend. I accepted her offer, and off we went.

We hadn't gone far when she said: 'You're lucky, you know. You happen to bump into me, I happen to like you, and Yolande happens to be back in Paris. You wouldn't have found her a few days ago. She was still in the country, recovering.'

'Recovering? From what?' I said.

'The chap whose mistress she was died at the beginning of the year. I don't know if she loved him, but it's always a shock – especially when it happens so tragically. He killed himself, and his wife. Désiris, his name was. Perhaps you heard about it?'

5 New angles

In the rue du Dobropol there were cars parked down both sides of the street, most of them smart two-seater convertibles, ideal for couples on summer excursions. They were painted in bright colours, probably to match their owners' underwear.

I followed Régine into one of those six-storey blocks that were considered modern during the Art Deco period. They were built on the site of the ancient fortifications, and the street names celebrate the Balkans expedition of 1915: Dobropol, Dardanelles, Salonica. We took the lift to a small but cosy flat on the third floor. It was warm inside, and there was a pleasant smell in the air.

'Sit down while I go and tidy up,' said Régine. 'Would you like something to drink? It's just the right time for an apéritif.'

She went over to a little bar and made me a drink. 'What about having lunch together?'

'I'd like that very much,' I said. 'But I've got work to do. I must see your friend Yolande.'

'She won't fly away,' said Régine. 'She lives upstairs, with Rita. I'll deal with all that in a minute.'

And she disappeared into the bathroom.

I took a swig of apéritif. Régine, Yolande, Rita . . . What names these dames had! I spotted a street directory under the telephone table, and opened it at Dobropol.

Rita Marson, Yolande Mège, Consuelo Mogador, Régine Monteuil . . . Arielle this, Léonor that, Chantal the other . . . One Marlene, two Doras . . . This block did have some tenants with ordinary names, but most of them preferred the exotic variety. Their real names were probably something like Marie or Jeanne . . .

But wasn't there some other oddity here? I ran my eye once again over this list of single but rarely unaccompanied girls. Rita Marson (the one Yolande lived with): telephone number NIEL 23–00. Yolande Mège herself: telephone number NIEL 34–45. What did that mean? Did Yolande really live with her girlfriend, or did she have a flat of her own? She seemed a rather complicated young lady.

I put the directory back and went to have a look out of the corner window. It faced on to the boulevard de Dixmude, on the far side of which stood a derelict factory. Once the name of the firm that owned it had been displayed in great bold letters along its walls, but now those walls were plastered with layers of tattered posters, and where any wall was visible the letters had worn away.

Further off, to the right, stretched Levallois-Perret, the domain of the car industry, now shrouded in November mist. And straight ahead, further away still, beyond Neuilly, was the Ile de la Grande-Jatte.

I thought of Désiris.

Suddenly I caught a subtle whiff of perfume. I sensed someone behind me and turned to find Régine. She had made her face up, fixed her hair, and poured herself into sheer nylon stockings and a dress with a breathtakingly low neckline. Poised there on her slender high heels, she looked infinitely desirable.

'Do you like me like this?' she said archly.

'Very much,' I said.

There's always a fly in the ointment. A distant siren began to moan, and others followed suit nearer at hand, until the whole of Paris and its suburbs seemed to be wailing desolately. It was midday on Thursday, 6 November, and on the first Thursday of every month our worthy administration checks its warning system. One way of announcing the lunch-break. Whets your appetite, so long as it's not for real.

'So, are we having lunch together?' she said.

'With pleasure. But first . . .'

'I know . . . Yolande.'

She picked up the telephone and dialled the number. 'Hello, Rita . . . It's Régine. Is Yolande there? Oh, really? All right, I'll ring back later.' She hung up. 'She's gone out and won't be back until quite late in the afternoon. Rita's got a visitor, you see. She always has a visitor on Thursday.' She gave a meaning smile. 'So Yolande's not there. We'll be able to take our time and have our lunch in peace. Shall we go?'

Later, as we were coming out of the restaurant, Régine said: 'If you've nothing better to do, come and have a *digestif*. I've got some excellent vodka.'

I accepted.

As we were walking towards the lift, a tall and elegant brunette emerged from it. A most alluring girl with smouldering black eyes. This must be Consuelo; she radiated Hispanic glamour at thirty paces.

'Hello, Ré,' she said, with an accent that confirmed

my suspicions. And off she clicked in her high heels. It sounded as if she was doing a Spanish tap-dance.

Régine and I got into the lift.

'What did she call you?' I asked, smiling.

'Ré. She always shortens people's names.'

'Her name's Consuelo Mogador, isn't it?'

'Yes. Do you know her?'

'No. I saw her name in the street directory just now.'

Back in Régine's flat we took off our coats and did honour to the famous vodka.

'So Yolande was Désiris's mistress – is that right?' I said.

'Yes.'

'He must have had plenty of money, then?'

'Of course,' she said. 'You should see the car he gave her! She's still got it. I know he worked in the business and got reductions, but still . . .'

She described the car. The latest Tallemet. Régine was a talkative girl. I'd probably pick a lot up from her.

'Did you know Désiris yourself?' I said.

'I was there when they first met. Consuelo was giving a little party at her place, I don't quite remember why. I think her boyfriend had brought off a deal or something. Désiris was there. So were Yolande and I.'

'So he was a friend of Mademoiselle Mogador, was he?'

'No. Of Monsieur Pierre, more like. Consuelo's friend.'

'Does Monsieur Pierre work in the car business too?'

'I don't know. He travels a lot.'

'Did you know Désiris well?'

'I saw him in the lift or on the stairs two or three times. Until Yolande moved out, that is. He must have thought we were all too much on top of one another here. Felt there wasn't enough privacy. So he rented a house in the rue Rochefort, near the parc Monceau. That shows he was well off. Not that he had the whole house, but old Madame Mèneval would have made him pay through the nose for the part he did have.'

'Who's Madame Mèneval?' I asked.

'Haven't you ever heard of Huguette Mèneval, or *de* Mèneval as she used to like to be called? In her day she was apparently the most successful *cocotte* in Paris.'

I smiled. 'That was before my time.'

It was Régine's turn to smile. 'Of course,' she said. 'I'm sorry . . . The Countess must be at least eighty.'

'Is she really a countess?'

'No. We just call her that.'

An aristocrat of the boudoir.

'Is she a friend of yours?' I said.

'We're all friends with her,' Régine said. 'She often pops in to see us. She says we remind her of her youth. She reads the cards for us, gives us advice, tells us how to handle our careers. Of course we don't listen to her. But she does make us laugh. Perhaps we're wrong, though – she certainly knew how to look after herself. Mark you, that's easy if you're as tight-fisted as she's always been!'

'Stingy, is she?' I said.

'Believe me, *she*'s never spent money like water! And some of her protectors were bankers and politicians. They say a leading cabinet minister once committed suicide because of her. It almost brought down the government. And she still has the house in the rue Rochefort, together with a tidy little nest-egg in cash and investments.'

I'm always fascinated by the lives of the great

courtesans, but I switched the conversation back to the subject of Yolande. 'About the suicide,' I said. 'Did Désiris bump himself off because of Yolande? Was she unfaithful to him?'

'No. She was more surprised than anyone. She read about it in the paper, and I know it gave her a real shock. You see, although she didn't live here any more, she and the Countess used to come and see us from time to time.'

'How come she didn't go to the police?' I said.

'Who?'

'Yolande.'

'What for?'

'To tell them she was his mistress.'

'What good would that have—' She stopped suddenly, and her face clouded. She took my hand and looked at me for a long time. There was a special kind of sadness in her eyes, as if I'd just let her down.

'What are you up to?' she said. Her voice was low, but full of reproach.

'Just asking questions,' I said.

'Yes,' she said, 'and I'm answering them.'

She let go of my hand, and when she spoke again her voice was shaking with suppressed anger. 'I'm doing more than answer them. I'm telling you things before you even ask – blathering on like an idiot! What was it you said you were?'

'A private investigator.'

'You mean a cop!'

'No, not a cop.'

She shrugged. 'Oh, what does it matter! It wasn't me who was sleeping with Désiris. Yolande will have to sort out her own problems. But I wouldn't want her to get into trouble because of me.'

'She won't get into trouble,' I said. 'I'm not a real cop. I know some of them, but I don't see why I should go and tell them Désiris kept a mistress who's now living in the rue du Dobropol. The suicide's ancient history now. The file's closed. And you're right – Yolande's testimony wouldn't have made any difference last March. And it might just have got her in trouble. Not serious trouble, but still, you never know with the police. That's what she thought, isn't it? And the rest of you agreed.'

'That's what the Countess advised.'

'And she's had some experience when it comes to suicide,' I said. 'Anyhow, let's forget that. All I meant was . . .'

I made a vague gesture and changed the subject, though my curiosity wasn't entirely satisfied.

Time passed. Night fell. It was time to see if Yolande was back. Régine telephoned again.

'Hello – is that you Yolande?' she said. 'Can I come up? I've got someone here who wants to offer you some work. Yes, that's it. We'll be right up.'

I grabbed my coat and was just ready to leave when Régine put a hand on my arm.

'We've been sitting next to each other for hours,' she said almost shyly, 'and you haven't even touched me.'

I smiled. 'Should I have?' I said.

She hesitated, then shook her head. 'No, I don't think so. But you deserve a reward.'

She pulled me to her and kissed me on the lips. She might have been shy the moment before, but she wasn't shy now. Not by a long shot. I kissed her in return and she responded again. It was too good to miss. I kissed her harder, and she reciprocated. And so on for some time. But we couldn't keep Yolande waiting for ever. So we broke it up.

6 *Yolande*

In real life, as I'd expected, Yolande was almost the
spitting image of Dany Darnys, and it hadn't taken
much artifice to enhance the resemblance. She did,
as I'd noticed when studying *P.P.T.*, have a more
developed bust – to put it mildly. It was straining
against her blouse, and a cheekily plunging neckline
revealed the most enticing of valleys, into which a pen-
dant on a little chain ventured from time to time as she
moved. The light danced in her golden hair and struck
fire from a stone on her finger.

After making the necessary introductions, Régine
told how I'd been looking for Yolande at Dupont's
studio, and what a heroic part I'd played there. Yolande
listened and looked at me, eyes wide with curiosity
between her long lashes.

'Right,' said Régine when she'd finished. 'I'm going
to leave you two together now. Be good.'

And with a swish of her skirt she vanished.

'Sit down, Monsieur Burma,' said Yolande.

I risked trying one of those modern contraptions that
look like anything but a chair, and to my surprise I
didn't fall off. Yolande sat down a little way off and lit
a fragrant cigarette.

'So you've been looking for me, have you?' she said at last.

'Yes.'

'What for?'

She sounded scared. Not of anything in particular, but as if she sensed danger.

'To offer you a job,' I said. 'It's well paid and not too exhausting.'

I brought out the magazine. 'Did you know,' I said, opening it at the appropriate pages, 'that you look just like the new film star – Dany Darnys?'

'So people say.'

'Almost the same face, the same figure, the same colour hair . . .'

'Oh, the hair's recent,' she admitted. 'To bring out the likeness. It was Didier's idea. He's a photographer at Dupont's.'

'The sex maniac?' I said.

'No. Another one. Dupont has several photographers working for him.'

That was enough about photographers and their obsessions. I wanted to get down to brass tacks. 'Right. Now listen, mademoiselle. I've come here on behalf of Dany Darnys. She believes you're doing her harm with these pictures, and she'll pay as much as is necessary for you to change your job. She's very serious about it, and would be prepared to take you on as her stand-in. It could be your chance to make a start in the cinema. You may only start as a stand-in, but there's nothing to stop Dany Darnys finding you a little role here and there. Anyway, it's better to have her on your side than against you. She's got a lot of pull now. Haven't you thought of going into the cinema before?'

'Oh yes, but . . .'

She seemed bowled over by my proposition. So I went through it all again, pointing out all its advantages, and finally she agreed.

'Good,' I said getting up. 'We must make an appointment. Do you mind if I use your phone?'

Dany Darnys wasn't at home, but the maid said I could try ELYSEES 26–19, and I got her there. When I gave her the news, together with Yolande's name and address, she congratulated me on my efficiency and said she couldn't wait to meet her double.

'You don't have to wait,' I said. 'I'm calling from her place, and you can meet her right away if you like.'

'No, not now,' she said. 'I'm busy . . . But I'll be home at about eleven tonight. Could you bring her then?'

'That should be possible,' I said. 'Just a minute.'

I consulted Yolande.

'Mademoiselle Mège agrees,' I told Dany.

'Perfect. See you tonight, then.'

We hung up.

'There you are!' I said to Yolande. 'Your fortune's as good as made!'

'So much the better,' she said. 'Things were beginning to get a bit tight.'

'Don't tell Dany Darnys that, whatever you do,' I said. 'Pretend you're rolling in it. Otherwise she'll palm you off with a pittance.'

She looked at me, running the tip of a pink tongue thoughtfully over her lips.

'You're a decent chap,' she said. 'Reliable, as well, I should think.'

'Isn't that what Régine just told you?' I said. 'I'm always ready to help a nice young girl.'

And pump her for information if necessary, too. I was rather disgusted with myself, but I couldn't get it out of my head that Désiris's suicide had been not the end but the beginning of some very funny business. And as I had his 'widow' sitting right in front of me . . .

'How about a drink?' Yolande suggested. 'To celebrate my new job. I hope it won't bring bad luck!'

'Don't be so superstitious,' I said. But she gave a nervous laugh as she prepared the drinks.

'To think that when Régine said you were looking for me I thought you must be one of the men who are supposed to have come and frightened Madame Mèneval!' she said, handing me my glass.

Well, well! Someone had been throwing a scare into the Countess, had they?

'Madame Mèneval?' I said. 'Who's she?'

She told me much the same as Régine had done.

'And someone frightened the poor old girl, did they?' I said.

'That's what she says.'

'Well, it wasn't me.'

'I don't doubt it,' she said, taking a sip of her drink. 'Anyhow, I was sure she was making it up.'

'Does she still go in for that kind of thing, at her age?' I said.

'I mean, it was an excuse for saying I had to leave. Mingy old cow!'

I tried not to look too interested.

'Excuse me,' I said, 'this is all rather complicated. Do you live with the old woman, or here?'

'I used to live at her place, but I left there to go to Nice. To work in the cinema, as a matter of fact. Try to, at least. I thought I might have more luck down there. But I didn't. I hope when I'm working for Dany Darnys . . .'

'Things will be better then!' I said. 'You mark my words.'

'I hope so,' she sighed. 'I was down on the Côte for several months. I left Paris about the middle of March and didn't get back till a couple of weeks ago. More or less broke.'

'I know what it's like,' I said. 'There's nothing to be ashamed of.'

She played with her ring, making the green stone flash. Memories, memories! She must have had a serious friendship down there which didn't last. Still, things could have been worse. It looked like a real emerald. If so, it was worth a small fortune.

'So I went back to Huguette's,' she went on. 'That's when she came out with the story about two thugs who'd come looking for me while I was away. She said they'd threatened her, and she still hadn't got over it. "If you're likely to have any more visitors like that," she said, "I'd rather you went and lived somewhere else." You see, like a fool I'd told her how broke I was, and she's so mean she made up any old excuse just to get rid of me. So I spent a few days in a hotel, then came to see Rita, and she kindly offered to put me up. This is her flat. I used to have one in this building too, but it's not free any more.'

'You're just as well off here,' I said. 'Madame Mèneval doesn't sound at all nice.'

'No, she isn't.'

'She must have made it all up, as you say. Unless you've got enemies.'

Her beautiful eyes widened. 'What do you mean?'

'Oh, I don't know,' I said. 'It was just an idea. Anyway, if she'd been as frightened as all that she'd have given the men your address in Nice, and they'd have turned up there.'

She shook her head. 'No one knew where I was,' she said. 'I was feeling so low I didn't keep in touch with anyone. I'd suffered a great loss, and I wanted to be alone.'

I didn't ask what the great loss had been because I knew already. Désiris. Perhaps this was a chance to bring him into the conversation, but I didn't feel close enough to Yolande to try it. Besides, I was in no hurry.

'Just a tall story then,' I said, as if dismissing the subject. 'What are you doing until eleven o'clock? If you're free, perhaps you and Régine and I can all have dinner together somewhere, and then go on and have a drink. What do you say?'

She thought it was a good idea. I intended to find out more while we were all gorging. I extricated myself from my peculiar chair.

'Do you mind organizing it with Régine,' I said, 'while I go and pick up my car? I left it on the boulevard Berthier.'

'Don't bother,' she said. 'We can take mine.'

'With pleasure,' I said. 'But I must move mine anyway.'

I went out into a drizzle typical of the time of year. On the corner of the boulevard Gouvion-St-Cyr I hailed a taxi – one of the taxis that at this time of the day make their way back to Levallois via the porte de Champerret. It was a short trip, but on the way I thought about the two men who'd scared the Countess. She hadn't made it up – they really existed. It was probably the same pair who'd attacked Dany Darnys, thinking she was Yolande. And they were after Yolande because she was Désiris's mistress – she'd obviously been telling the truth when she said she had no enemies of her own. I had plenty to think about.

My car was still where I'd left it that morning, before going into the *Purely Parisian Thrills* office. The windscreen was festooned with tickets, but so what? It would collect a few more between now and midnight. I got in and started up.

A little later I was leaving the car in the avenue de Wagram, not far from Dany Darnys's house – parking area or no parking area. Then I took another taxi back to the rue du Dobropol, where Régine and Yolande were waiting.

'Where are we having dinner?' I asked.

'Bistro 22 in the avenue Niel – is that all right?' said Yolande, covering her hair with a scarf as way-out as her furniture.

Bistro 22 was OK by me. I'd known it when Weinuc, its original owner, once a painter, was still alive.

The girls put on their fur coats, and down we went.

Yolande's Tallemet convertible was as impressive as Régine had suggested. Even if Désiris had got it at a discount, it must have made a hole in his cheque-book. Yolande put her in gear and we were off. Lucky old Nestor, spinning along in a cloud of costly perfume, wedged between two pairs of the softest, most hospitable thighs in Paris!

Our arrival in the restaurant caused quite a stir. Whether they were eating their dinner or goggling at the pictures that covered the walls, the customers all stopped and stared at us. I looked just like a gangster out with two of his molls. But it was Yolande who attracted the most attention. Everyone must have thought she was Dany Darnys. As I pointed out after we'd been shown to a table in a quiet corner, underneath a snow scene.

'You should have seen Dany's face when she looked at those photos,' I added later on, as we were tucking in. 'She was *not* happy, I can tell you!'

Yolande blinked. 'Are you really sure she wants to do me a good turn?' she asked anxiously.

'Quite sure,' I said.

'She's not going to be furious with me for having worked for Dupont?'

'Not if you promise never to pose as her again. That's all she asks.'

'It's not Yolande's fault if she looks like someone else,' put in Régine.

'I didn't even realize it myself,' said Yolande. 'It was Didier, the photographer, who pointed it out. I needed to earn some money when I got back to Paris, and as I'd worked for Dupont earlier on . . .' She hesitated.

'Before Désiris started to keep you,' I thought.

'. . . I went to his studio to see if there was anything doing there.'

Didier had wanted to know where she'd got to. He'd been looking for her for weeks. (She'd been in general demand, apparently!) He'd noticed there was a resemblance between her and the new star, and he and Dupont, always on the look out for a fiddle, had realized there was money to be made out of it. Yolande had played along, and they'd been so pleased with the result they'd completely re-vamped the next edition to include her pictures.

'I won't deny I took to the idea,' Yolande said, 'and I've been cultivating the resemblance ever since.'

'Well, Mademoiselle Darnys will certainly ask you to drop it and go back to looking your old self,' I said. 'It's in your own interests, anyway, if you want to work in the cinema too.'

'Of course.'

We talked a bit about Didier. Apparently he was a very decent bloke, nothing like the lout who'd tried to rape Régine that morning. This reminded me of something. I decided to fly a kite.

'Decent bloke or not, Didier doesn't seem up to much as an artist,' I said. 'Or perhaps it's a defect in his camera. When I was looking at the photographs, I noticed a mark on the inside of one of your thighs, and it didn't look like a fault in the developing or printing.'

'You really did give those pictures the once over!' the two girls hooted. No false modesty there.

'The fault was in the model, that's all,' Yolande explained good-naturedly, when she'd recovered from her hilarity. 'I've got this nasty scar that you simply can't hide with make-up.'

She explained how as a child she'd almost impaled herself getting over a gate. And as she spoke I understood what the two men who attacked Dany Darnys had been up to. They'd had no intention of raping her. When they saw her they must have doubted whether she was really Yolande, so they'd proceeded to check to see if she had Yolande's distinctive mark.

At any rate, *I* was no longer in doubt: there were two unsavoury characters – thugs according to Dany Darnys, frightening according to Huguette Mèneval – roving about Paris and trying to find Yolande. But I still had no idea why. I wondered whether I should tell her about them, or just keep an eye on her until they turned up again a third time. I decided to leave it until after Yolande's meeting with Dany Darnys. Because there was something that didn't tie up there, either.

We talked of this and that until the end of the meal, and then went and had a drink in a quiet little bar in the rue Bayen. At one point I tried to call Zavatter, but I had no luck at either his home or any of his usual haunts. I telephoned Hélène at her place, but she had no news of him either. The time eventually came for our appointment with Dany Darnys.

All three of us went in to see her.

'Here's your double – Mademoiselle Mège,' I said to the actress, who was looking at Yolande with immense curiosity. 'Don't scold her for her past artistic activities. She's willing to cooperate.'

Soon afterwards, Régine and I slipped out and left the other two to have their chat in peace. Officially, my job was over, and Yolande was old enough to see herself home. I explained to Régine that I'd left my car near by.

'Where are we going?' she asked as we got in.

'Just for the moment,' I said, lighting my pipe and offering her a Gitane, 'we'll wait here, if you don't mind.'

'Not at all!' she said with a mocking laugh. She obviously thought I just wanted to show her what a keen private eye I was. I wasn't going to disillusion her.

The drizzle had been succeeded by a slight fog, which drew haloes round the neon signs outside cinemas and restaurants. But visibility was still good, and from where I was sitting I could see the entrance to Dany Darnys's house, and Yolande's car a little way down the street.

As I chatted to Régine and kept a weather eye open,

I was also thinking. Dany Darnys had seemed to be alone, but I had a feeling there was company about. Maybe whoever it was had slipped out when we arrived, or perhaps they wouldn't show up until later. At any rate, I was determined to wait until Yolande came out. Then we'd see.

A good hour went by. Nobody went into the house and nobody came out. Then at last the front door opened and Yolande emerged. Alone. I didn't know whether I was disappointed or relieved. She went towards her car, climbed in and drove off.

I started my engine. 'So there we are,' I said. 'That seems to be all for today. Shall I take you home?' I asked.

'If you like.'

She seemed to have gone off me a bit. Probably because she thought I was showing off.

I kept on the Tallemet's tail for a few minutes, then lost it, and didn't pick it up again until I came round the corner of the boulevard Gouvion-St-Cyr and saw it parked beside the pavement in the rue du Dobropol. Yolande was just getting out.

The street was completely deserted. The shrubs planted around the apartment blocks threw shadows too deep for the light from the street-lamps to penetrate. Here and there the glow from a window served only to make the the whole scene seem darker and more lonely.

All for today? Come on, Nestor. Don't be defeatist!

Suddenly Régine clutched my arm. She was so panic-stricken I could feel her nails right through my sleeve.

She had seen it, too.

Two men had emerged from the shadows and were

swiftly approaching Yolande. It happened so fast there wasn't a hope of stopping them. Something gleamed in the dark – more likely a revolver than a cosh – and a blow on the back of the head folded her into the arms of one of her assailants. She didn't make a sound. And even as this was happening, I turned towards Régine and clapped my hand over her mouth to stop her from screaming.

7 *Levallois by night*

When I looked back up the street the figures had disappeared. Then the Tallemet started up and roared away in the direction of Levallois. I let go of Régine and set off in pursuit.

'Oh my God!' she moaned. 'What's happening?'

I patted her on the thigh to reassure her, but couldn't tell if it had done any good. For the moment it was the best I could manage.

'You saw what happened,' I said. 'Just like I did.'

'They've kidnapped Yolande!' she said. Her voice was ominously high-pitched.

'Yes,' I said.

'They're white slavers, aren't they?'

'I don't know.'

'Why didn't you do something?'

She was getting aggressive; the last stage before hysteria.

'Because there was nothing I could do,' I said. 'It was no use trying to play the hero. It makes more sense to find out where they're going. Now for God's sake get off my back! I haven't got time to chat.'

She huddled up in the corner of her seat.

I took out my gun and put it between us like the sword between Tristan and Isolde, though here the intention was different. I like to be prepared for anything.

'You've got a gun, and you still let them get away with it!' said Régine.

'Shut up!' I said.

I didn't hear another squeak out of her.

While all this was going on, the Tallemet had taken the boulevard de l'Yser at a good lick, turned into the rue Caran d'Ache and crossed the avenue de la porte de Champerret. So far so good. They didn't seem to have spotted me. I recognized the streets and knew more or less the direction we were going in. But it didn't last. As we reached the heart of Levallois and its maze of ill-lit, badly cobbled streets, I began to lose my bearings. The car's suspension groaned under the hammering it was taking. So did Régine as she was bounced from side to side. By now Yolande's kidnappers must have realized they were being tailed. They began to try to shake me off, and I zigzagged after them, screeching round corners and hurling the car right and left as I reacted to their sudden changes of direction. This wasn't my first car chase, and the distance between us didn't widen.

Suddenly a hard object was jammed into my ribs. It might have been a pipe-stem but it wasn't. 'Turn back now,' said Régine tonelessly. 'I'm scared.'

Scared wasn't the word for it. She was so terrified I could feel it. Despite her make-up and the feebleness of the light from the dashboard, I could see she was deathly pale, and now really on the verge of hysterics.

I took a quick look at my gun. It was too dark to

see if the safety catch was on, and I couldn't remember how I'd left it when I'd put it on the seat. What I *could* see quite clearly, however, was that her finger was on the trigger and that it was trembling terribly. If the catch was off and her finger shook too much, it wouldn't be long before I got a slug right in the bread basket. In the state she was in it wouldn't be wise to argue.

I swore and stopped the car. Out in front a winking indicator faded into the fog. An ironic goodnight from the Tallemet.

'Silly idiot,' I said.

I took advantage of the fact that, from fatigue or nervousness, she'd let the barrel of the gun droop. I grabbed at it and ripped it out of her hand.

She gave me a frenzied look, then her mouth twisted and opened slowly to let out a noise not unlike the wail of the sirens at midday. I didn't like the look of this. I slapped her several times, as much to give vent to my own anger at her untimely interference as to nip her hysteria in the bud. She went completely limp, and almost slid off the seat on to the floor. Well, let her faint if she felt like it. That way she'd be out of my hair. But instead of fainting she started to sob.

I put the gun back in my pocket and climbed out of the car. Cobbles had given way to asphalt. The poorly lit street was deserted. On either side, little terraced houses were plunged in sleep. I didn't know Levallois all that well, and now I felt completely lost. At my approach a frightened cat leapt out of a dustbin and fled. From far away, muffled by the fog, came the familiar sound of a fire-engine. Gradually it died away, and the night was quiet again. I came out into a wider street. The rue Gide. Was it named after Charles, the economist, or André, the writer? There was no way of knowing. All the Gides could go to hell. Shivering in the damp night air, I went back to the car.

Régine was still hunched up in the corner where I'd left her, dabbing at her nose with a handkerchief.

'I've still got one or two things to do around here,' I said, holding the door open. 'If you don't like it you can get out and leg it home.'

She didn't answer, which I took to mean she preferred to stay, so I got back behind the wheel and took off. There was no real point now in trying to find the Tallemet. But I might be lucky. Anyhow, what I needed most was to calm down. I drove furiously all over Levallois, checking on every car that was anything like Yolande's. In vain. I realized I was going round in circles, and came to a stop in front of a Métro station where the metal barrier was just being rolled down for the night. Above the steps going down into the tunnel was the name: *Louise-Michel.* I was back on the outskirts of Paris. I headed for the rue du Dobropol.

Régine was snivelling louder than ever, but managed to whisper: 'I'm sorry about just now. But I was so frightened! I thought: "We're going to catch up with them, and then what will happen?"'

I'd already gathered she hadn't wanted to get involved in a fight, and despite the anger I'd felt at the time I couldn't really blame her. On the contrary, the more I thought about it the more I realized she'd given me a good excuse for giving up, without losing face, a chase that was doomed to disaster. So long as the kidnappers hadn't known they were being followed I'd had the advantage of surprise. But once they'd spotted me it was different. In short, Régine had stopped me from tackling them in even more unpromising circumstances than if I'd jumped them at the beginning.

'Don't worry,' I said. 'Forget it.' And I patted her on the thigh. It could become a habit, but I could think of less pleasurable ones.

When we got back to the rue du Dubropol the only parking space I could find was some way beyond Régine's block. She got out first, her high heels echoing loudly over the pavement as I started walking her to her door.

A car door slammed with a noise like a gunshot. Régine started, and my hand went to my revolver. I looked around to see where the sound had come from. On the other side of the street a man had climbed out of a car. It looked as if he'd been waiting for someone. He was just a shape in the shadows until he lit a cigarette – slowly, so that the flame of his lighter played on his face.

It was Roger Zavatter. I hadn't been expecting to see *him*.

Régine was showing signs of apprehension.

'It's only a mate of mine,' I said. 'Hello, Roger,' I called, to show him it was all right to approach us.

He crossed over, his hands in the pockets of his car coat. As he came up he raised a finger to the peak of his check cap in a casual salute to Régine.

'What the hell are you doing here?' I said.

'Waiting for someone,' he said. 'Someone you asked me to take an interest in.'

'Marcel Viénot?'

'The very same.'

Strangely enough, this didn't altogether surprise me. 'Is he in the area?'

'In there,' he said, pointing to Régine's building.

'How long's he been there?'

'Five minutes.'

'We'd better . . .' I began, but stopped.

A light had just appeared in the hall. Through the glass door we could dimly hear the hum of the lift descending.

'Look out,' I said, 'that may be him. Get back in your car, Roger. If it is him, follow him. If you find out where he lives or anything else of interest call me at . . .'

I turned to Régine. 'What's your number?' I said.

'NIEL 78–69.'

'Got it,' said Zavatter.

He walked back to his car, and the sound of his getting in blended with that of the lift doors clanging to. I pulled Régine towards me and clasped her in my arms as a smartly dressed, well-built fellow of about forty came out of the building. With barely a glance at the couple of lovers smooching near by, he walked a little way down the street and climbed into a car. When he started the engine Zavatter's car started up too.

'Let's go,' I said.

Back in her flat Régine tried to make a joke of it: 'Well, one certainly never gets bored in your company,' she said. But her heart wasn't in it. She was still scared.

'You bet,' I said.

'What does it all mean?' she said tearfully, putting a hand on my arm. 'Yolande . . . ?'

'Don't worry,' I said. 'We'll find her. What's the registration number of her car?'

'2107 AB 75.'

I called the Levallois police station.

'Hello,' I said. 'Something suspicious to report, chief.'

'Yeah?' grunted a copper who didn't seem at all flattered by this promotion. 'What?'

He'd obviously been quite happy playing cards.

'A couple of men have been seen molesting a young woman in the rue Gide,' I said. 'They were in a Tallemet, registration number 2107 AB 75.'

'Who's speaking?'

I hung up. It was over to them now. A bit later I rang again and repeated what I'd said before. It might make them think again if they'd taken no notice the first time. But I wasn't too sure.

'So what do you think, now you've seen a private detective on the job?' I said, just about managing a smile, though it was the last thing I felt like.

'Well, it was only the first time,' she said.

'You haven't seen anything yet,' I told her. 'Which reminds me, we *didn't* see Yolande being kidnapped, all right? The last time we set eyes on her was when we left her at Dany Darnys's place. You won't forget that?'

'No.'

Later on Zavatter called.

'He's gone home, and I don't think he'll go out again now,' he said. 'He lives on the boulevard des Batignolles, near the Hébertot Theatre. What do I do?'

'Stay where you are,' I said. 'Where are you calling from?'

'A few yards from my car,' he said, 'and about the same distance from Viénot's place. I'm in a phone box, and there's a gale blowing.'

'I'll be right there,' I said.

'All right – spill it,' I told Zavatter as I climbed in next to him.

Beyond the misted windscreen the multicoloured neon lights of the Place Clichy flicked on and off in the darkness.

'Well,' said Zavatter, 'just over thirty hours ago you asked me to get what information I could on Dany Darnys and a friend of hers called Viénot. And, in all modesty, I doubt if I've ever picked up so much dope in so little time!'

'You'll have your reward,' I said. 'Now get to the point.'

'Thank you. Well, I started with the easiest – the actress. Not much to say about her. Generally considered to be a dumb blonde, makes a pig's ear of it when she tries to help promote her own image. Last October she invented a story about being attacked—'

'I know,' I said. 'Except that she didn't invent it.'

'Oh?'

'No. But that's only a detail – the rest seems to fit. Brainless, is she?'

'Chivalry apart, yes.'

'Suggestible? Could she be manipulated without realizing it?'

'Definitely.'

'Just as I thought. Now what about Viénot?'

'A quiet type,' said Zavatter. 'Intelligent. I gathered it was him you were most interested in, so I stuck with him. He's forty. A snappy dresser. You saw him, anyway.'

'I caught a glimpse,' I said.

'He's got a senior research job with Roger Richard's, the car people. He used to work for Dugat – maybe he

met your man Désiris there. He's been in favour with
Dany Darnys ever since she became famous. I followed
him this evening when he left work. I recognized him
from what people had told—'

'Get on with it,' I said.

'He came home here first, then went to a restaurant,
and after that to a bar. If you want the addresses . . .'

'No, thanks.'

'He spoke to two or three people during the evening,
but nothing out of the way.'

'Did he make any phone calls?'

'Several. But he can't have got through to whoever
it was he wanted, because he always looked pretty fed
up afterwards. But at about nine o'clock, in the bar,
he must have had more luck, because he came up from
the phone booth looking quite pleased. Not over the
moon, but pleased. Then he went into what I thought
was deep meditation, but in fact he must have been
trying to remember what films were on, because when
he left the bar he went to a cinema on the Champs-
Elysées. When he came out of there he went and had
a leisurely drink, made another phone call, and drove
to Dany Darnys's place.'

'What time was that?'

'After midnight,' said Zavatter. 'I went on waiting
outside – I don't know why, because if they were in
the sack together there wasn't much point. But he came
out again at about one, just as I was about to call it a
day. I tailed him again, and you know the rest: the rue
de Dobropol and so on.'

'Very good!' I said.

'What shall I do now?' he asked, with a yawn that
almost dislocated his jaw.

'Stay here,' I said. 'I'm going to call him from a bar, and maybe we'll go up to his place afterwards.'

I got into my car again and drove to the café on the corner of the Place Clichy and the rue Biot, where I looked up Viénot's number in the directory. He picked up the receiver at the first ring.

'Hello,' he said in a bright, wide-awake voice. It was as if he'd been waiting for a call.

'Nestor Burma speaking,' I said.

'Nestor Burma?' He was really surprised.

'Yes,' I said. 'I'm just down the road. I know it's late, but I'd like to talk to you.'

'Er . . . What about?'

'Yolande Mège and Charles Désiris.'

'Oh!' he said with a resigned laugh. 'All right. I'll be expecting you. Fourth floor – on the left as you get out of the lift.'

It was as simple as that.

He didn't look too pleased when he saw there were two of us, but invited us in politely. The room was full of period furniture: a sideboard, a round table and elaborately carved wooden chairs. Probably heirlooms.

He had a strong face, full of character, with a high forehead and crew-cut grey hair. His expression was one of slight annoyance, as of someone whose bluff has been called, though this was tempered by the cynicism of the good loser. But there was no hint of apprehension. He was wearing slippers, but still had his trousers on under his dressing gown.

'Was that you following me?' he asked, after offering us a seat and taking one himself.

'Following you?' I said. 'When?'

'Let's not play games, Monsieur Burma,' he said.

'When I started my car up in a certain street a little while ago, I noticed another car starting up at the same time. So I assume I was being followed . . .'

'Quite right,' I said, smiling. 'You *were* being trailed from the rue du Dobropol to the boulevard des Batignolles. But you were being followed before that as well – ever since you came out of the Roger Richard factory. By this gentleman—' I pointed at Zavatter with my pipe.

'On my instructions he's been gathering information about you, and he's scarcely let you out of his sight. Why? I don't want to play games either – it's late, and we're all too tired to beat about the bush – so I'll tell you why. It occurred to me that the person who recommended me to Dany Darnys – you – must have done so for his own purposes: he wanted to get his hands on Désiris's mistress without coming out into the open, and he was counting on Dany herself to make it possible. Left to herself, Dany probably wouldn't have bothered trying to stop her "double" from posing half-naked in a cheap magazine. But if someone with a persuasive enough manner suggested it, after you'd sent her a copy of the magazine through the post . . . Have I hit the nail on the head, Monsieur Viénot?'

'Precisely,' he said with a shrug.

'But why all the play-acting, for God's sake?'

'You've just explained why,' he said. 'I wanted to keep out of the limelight – to avoid letting people know I was interested in Yolande Mège. I didn't even know her name until this evening, when Dany told me.'

'The trouble is,' I said, 'you're going to have to come clean with me.'

'Dammit!' he said. 'Why did I tell Dany to go to

you? Someone else might not have dug all this up.'

'Someone else might not have dug up Yolande so fast, either.'

'That's true,' he said. 'Anyway, what's done is done. But why have you been going to all this trouble?'

'Maybe because I was mixed up in Désiris's suicide.'

He stared. 'Mixed up in . . .' he began.

'I discovered the body,' I said. 'My name was in the papers.'

He snapped his fingers. 'That's it! Hell! It must have stuck in my mind and I remembered it inadvertently when I was advising Dany to hire a private detective. How stupid—'

'Yes,' I said, 'but it shows you're telling me the truth.'

However devious he was, he'd hardly have chosen me deliberately because I'd found the bodies in the rue Alphonse-de-Neuville.

'Right,' I said. 'Let's see what we've got so far. You and Désiris knew one another, I suppose? You both worked at Dugat's.'

'Yes.'

'But you must have lost touch for a time.'

'Yes. When I left Dugat's in 1956.'

'How did you find out Yolande was his mistress?'

'I met him twice by chance this January, and he was with a young woman. It was Yolande, but I didn't know her name at the time. Maybe he introduced her and I forgot. Anyway, I was struck by how beautiful she was, and by her style. Rather different from his wife, who wasn't very . . . attractive.'

'You knew Madame Désiris, then?'

'By sight. Désiris and I were working together at the time when he got married.'

'Right,' I said. 'And you must have heard about it, in March, when he committed suicide.'

'Of course.'

'What did you make of it?'

'Nothing particular.'

'Then, in October the papers were full of pictures of a new actress who'd just starred in two films. And didn't you think Dany Darnys must be none other than Désiris's ex-mistress?'

'Yes.'

'And you set out to get to know her.'

'Yes.'

'Had you fallen for her?'

'No.'

'Why did you want to meet her, then?'

Viénot smiled. 'As if you didn't know.'

'The invention, eh?'

'That's right. You see, I'd worked with Désiris, and I realized what a good engineer he was. Brilliant. Full of ideas. But in the past his bosses had taken advantage of him, and he'd become bitter and secretive. But the ideas must have gone on churning away in his brain. I knew that article in the *Crépuscule* had got it all wrong. It said he'd killed himself because he'd run out of ideas and couldn't finish his project. Balderdash!'

'Why else might he have killed himself?' I asked.

'I've no idea. But that certainly wasn't the reason.'

'So you believe this invention existed?'

'I'm certain of it.'

I laughed. 'And that being the case, you said to yourself: "If I know Désiris, he completed the designs but was too suspicious to patent the whole thing. The key factors of it must be hidden in some safe place.

Perhaps his mistress could give me a clue to its where-abouts. At any rate, it won't cost me anything to try."
Is that it, M. Viénot?'

'Exactly. Except that it cost me a lot. Getting to know a girl like Dany Darnys is hideously expensive.'

'But it was worth it, wasn't it?' I said.

He didn't answer.

'The trouble was,' I went on. 'Dany Darnys wasn't who you thought she was.'

He nodded.

'You realized that as soon as you saw her close to,' I said. 'She and Yolande are alike, but not so much that you could mix them up if you examined them carefully. All the same, you went on seeing her.'

'Dany is very pleasant company,' he explained, preening himself slightly. 'And I might as well get some return for all the time and money I'd spent . . . Some compensation for my disappointment.'

'I see what you mean,' I said. 'That takes us up to the last few days. You noticed the photos of Yolande in the latest number of *P.P.T.*, either by chance or because you're a regular reader. *Honi soit*, etc.! This time you were sure it was Désiris's mistress, but you didn't know how to find out where she lived. A private detective was what you needed. So you sent Dany a copy of the magazine, persuaded her she had to stop Yolande, and said you'd heard of a smart detective called Nestor Burma.'

'I was right there,' he laughed.

'Thank you . . . So I found Yolande and told Dany, who told you. Now, you could have been there when the two women met, but you were afraid Yolande would recognize you and start talking about Désiris.'

'Yes,' he said. 'And I'd have had to explain. That would have complicated things.'

'It certainly would. Dany Darnys may not be all that bright, but she'd certainly have realized you'd mistaken her for Yolande. What's more, if Désiris's name had been mentioned she'd have remembered what her two mysterious attackers had said back in October. Especially as I talked to her about it only yesterday.'

I checked my watch. 'The day before yesterday, rather. Yes, that certainly would have caused complications. Which reminds me – it wasn't you who sent those thugs, was it?'

He protested.

'I only ask because it's best to get everything clear,' I said. 'Well, there seems to be some competition around, doesn't there? Could some other people in the car industry have followed the same line of reasoning as you, and be looking for the designs of Désiris's invention?'

He frowned. 'It's possible,' he said. 'Probable, even. I don't like the sound of that attack any more than you do. That's why I rushed straight round to Yolande's house tonight, even though it was so late. The thing is, if she does know something, it'll be a matter of first come first served. But she wasn't in. At least that's what the friend she shares a flat with . . . er . . .'

He took a notebook out of his pocket.

'Rita Marson . . . At least, that's what Rita Marson said. She wouldn't open the door. I slipped my visiting card under it, just in case.'

I relit my pipe. 'You've no idea who it could be?' I said.

'Who what could be?'

'The people in the car industry who might be stalking the same game as you.'

'I've no idea.'

'Well,' I said, 'it's none of my business.'

He burst out laughing. 'It may be none of your business, but you're pretty interested in it all the same!'

'But I meant what I said,' I told him. 'Appearances may be against me, but I never meddle in other people's affairs. But it *is* my business to clear up any odd details that crop up in a case I'm investigating, so that I don't get led up the garden by clients who think they can manipulate me. Some smart alecs do try! You, for instance. Why didn't you just come and see me and say frankly, "I want the name and address of this model", instead of faking all that scenario with Dany Darnys? But of course, you told me – you wanted to stay in the background. Why?'

'The fact is,' he said, 'it may seem rather childish, but I was afraid people would wonder why I was running after Désiris's ex-mistress.'

'To put it in a nutshell,' I said, 'you didn't want anyone suspecting it might have been the invention you were after.'

'Exactly.'

'If you find out anything from Yolande, you mean to claim the invention as your own, don't you?'

He fidgeted around on his chair.

'You put it very crudely,' he said.

'Whether I blurt it out or wrap it up,' I answered, 'it comes to the same thing. Don't think I want to preach. Once I'm sure you're not trying to trick *me*, the rest is no concern of mine. Dany Darnys paid me to find Yolande for her, and I've done it. As far as I'm concerned the case is closed. If you can manage to get something out of Yolande, good luck to you.'

'But get *what* out of her?' I thought. 'And when? Always assuming she does know something. And where have those other thugs taken her at this hour of the night?'

'Right,' I said. 'That's all. Good night, Monsieur Viénot.' I stood up. The other two followed suit. Zavatter was yawning.

'Good night, messieurs,' said Viénot.

He held out his hand and we both shook it. He had the firm, cordial handshake of an honest man. The kind there are so many of. The kind who look askance at you if you get into debt, or don't vote, or don't take your hat off when a funeral goes by, or decline to pass judgement on the concierge's daughter if she sleeps with the painter on the sixth floor. They've no time for anarchists and such-like! They're content to fiddle their taxes, cheat the customs, give short weight, or steal the results of a dead inventor's sleepless nights. Decent, respectable citizens. The world's full of them.

That's why it sometimes doesn't smell too good.

8 Breaking new ground

It was the same thing over and over again. It came in, receded, and then returned, with the quiet relentlessness of waves breaking on a beach.

I'd buy a spicy magazine at a news-stand, and no sooner did I open it than it turned into a technical review full of graphs and abstruse diagrams. But these were enlivened by animated cartoons of a scantily clad Yolande being pursued by rods and wheels and valves and pistons – machinery of all kinds, which finally overtook and buried her. Then I'd wake up. And a few minutes later, go back to sleep, buy a spicy magazine at a news-stand . . .

And so on until nine o'clock in the morning, when I reckoned it would be less exhausting to get up. Then, after I'd shaved and dressed, I'd be able to light my pipe and try to get rid of my hangover.

Some hope.

It was Friday, 7 November. The weather was gloomy. So was I. I was thinking about Yolande.

After introducing her to Dany Darnys and seeing how that turned out, I'd intended to keep a friendly eye on her . . . to protect her from the danger hanging over her because of the two men looking for her. But I'd been overtaken by events.

God, those thugs must be barmy! Yolande didn't know any more about Désiris's invention than I did. They'd soon realize that, and let her go. Maybe she was back at her friend's flat already. That's it! They'd let her go, with apologies. Just their style! Look how politely they'd invited her to go with them the night before. A couple of biffs on the back of the head with a revolver butt.

Let her go, indeed! Wake up, Burma.

I went into the kitchen for a glass of water. Then I drove to the office to see if there was a map of Levallois lying around somewhere. I found one covering both Levallois and Neuilly and, more to keep myself occupied than anything else, pencilled in as accurately as I could the route the kidnappers had taken from the rue du Dobropol in the XVIIth arrondissement to the rue Gide in Levallois, where I'd lost them.

Sherlock Holmes stuff. All I needed now was the colour of their hair and the ringleader's age, and I'd know where the Tallemet had been heading. I really did have some great ideas first thing in the morning! I was just about to chuck the map aside when something in the upper half of it caught my eye. There, lying between the two arms of the Seine like a lazy slug, was the Ile de la Grande-Jatte.

Maybe it was another crazy idea . . .

The yellow waters of the Seine rolled by, iridescent here and there with long streaks of oil. Between the leafless trees, with their lower branches trailing in the water, I could see an open-air café on stilts, together with a boat-house and the skeleton of an arbour that must have had flowers growing over it in summer. Two boats rocked back and forth, tugging at their moorings. But under the grey sky this humble holiday spot looked unspeakably dreary. Unless it was the effect of my hangover and my sombre thoughts. A black barrel anchored in the middle of the river served as a kind of buoy, dividing the current around it and occasionally trapping dead branches and bits of refuse. The thud of machinery came from an unseen factory. All that was missing, to complete the picture, was a dead dog. No doubt I could have found one if I looked.

I could come back if necessary. For the moment what I was looking for was Désiris's workshop. I had no idea where it could be, nor whether it was a large place or just a little shed. But the Ile de la Grand-Jatte isn't all that big. Somebody must remember him. Especially as he committed suicide!

But before asking any questions I wandered about a bit, prospecting. In the rue Benjamin-Constant a few places looked possible, but they were all occupied by ordinary artisans, whistling as they worked. Not that that meant anything: Désiris's place might have been rented out again since his death. But I didn't think it would have been.

I walked back the way I'd come and explored the boulevard de Levallois, inspecting in turn the premises of a coachbuilder, a maker of security devices, one specialist in springs and another specialist in gear boxes. This was ridiculous.

I went into a bistro wedged between a car uphol-sterer's and a soldering shop. It turned out to be the one I'd seen earlier. The open-air part, looking out on the river, was on the other side of the roughcast wall behind the bar. The barmaid was the Lollobrigida type with a touch of the Bardots in her pout. It's an epidemic. I ordered something for my dry throat, and we struck up a conversation about the weather. Finally I asked her if she knew of a workshop to let – I'd been told I'd find what I was after here on the island. Someone had mentioned the name of a bloke who'd had one, but who'd died. Désiris. Had she ever heard of him?

'Yes,' she said, 'but I don't know if the workshop's to let.'

'Where is it?'

'Right at the end of the island, on the boulevard Vital-Bouhot. You can't miss it – it's a kind of black wooden shed. It's got the name of the man who used to own it painted on the side – Dupleix.'

I made tracks.

The workshop in question stood on its own, separated from its nearest neighbours – a scrapyard and a garage – not only by a line of trees but also by a patch of waste ground strewn with junk of all descriptions. It was an evil-looking place, resembling most factories and workshops in that all the panes in its one window and in the fanlight over the door were either dirty or smashed. The name of the one-time owner was daubed on the front in sinister red. Only DUP was legible – the rest had been eaten away by time and weather. The shed stood some way from the street, at the end of a drive full of ruts and bordered with battered-looking bushes. At the other end of the drive, the wooden gate that once closed the place in now hung uselessly on its one remaining hinge.

While I was standing contemplating this scene, something brushed against my leg. It was a dog, come to sniff out what I was up to on its territory, and probably to beg for something to eat, too. It had the prosperous look you always see in animals fed on bolts and gaskets. It waited a bit, then went off looking disappointed. To jump in the river, probably.

I walked up the drive.

The front door of the workshop was firmly pad-locked. I wasn't going to get in that way. Reconnoitring round the back, I found another door that proved more cooperative. All I had to do was lift up the hatch and walk in.

The place wasn't any more thrilling inside than out. But there was more dust. Apart from a couple of expensive-looking machines, each welded on to a steel base, there was nothing that could have cost Désiris much. Even if he'd bought the place it wouldn't have ruined him. He hadn't spent much on upkeep, either. A third of the floor was concrete, a third was boarded over, and the rest was just beaten earth. The whole place exuded a dreadful feeling of neglect, which the semi-darkness did nothing to improve. I found a switch. Nix. Too bad! I'd have to do without light. What would I need it for, anyway?

In one corner there was a sort of glassed-in cubby-hole. I went inside. This must have been where the research went on. There was a drawing-board with rulers and compasses. Several set squares and T-squares hung on the walls. The rest of the equipment consisted of a desk with one drawer open, a filing cabinet, two chairs and a rickety stool.

But there were other things as well. Things that proved someone had been here. And not long ago.

Two bottles were standing on the table: one had

contained some kind of alcohol, and the other had an almost burned-out candle stuck in the neck. A lot of cigarette ends, varying in length, lay scattered on the floor, and on the floor under the table was something that looked like a cloth. It was a scarf. A scarf with a familiar pattern on it. The scarf Yolande had been wearing when she was kidnapped.

I picked it up. It was in a pitiful state, smeared with lipstick and torn in several places as if by teeth.

I sat down, nervously twisting the wretched scrap of silk around my fingers, not knowing what to think. Or rather, knowing only too well. This cubby-hole must have witnessed a very particular kind of get-together the night before. As I stared around, not taking in what I was seeing, I saw something protruding from under the filing cabinet: a cylindrical length of wood. I stared at it for some time before it dawned on me it was the handle of some sort of tool. I went and picked it up.

It was a shovel, with earth still clinging to the blade. I ran my finger over it, too shaken to be objective, unable to tell whether the earth was dry or damp.

I went out of the cubby-hole and strode back and forth in the workshop like a bear in a cage, bumping into a portable stove and sending it flying with a kick the next time I came by. I don't know how long it was before I realized I still had Yolande's scarf clutched in one hand and the shovel in the other. I threw down the scarf, but kept the shovel. Where I was standing the earthen floor was broken and uneven, as if it had been dug up and filled in again.

Time to get to work. Until now my corpses had been served up to me on a platter. All I'd had to do was wrap them up and pack them off to the morgue. This time I was going to have to do some grave-digging. Very good for me. Everybody should have more than one trade!

I went and made sure the door was shut, took off my coat and jacket, grasped the shovel in a none too steady hand and drove it at the floor. I was so worked up I didn't realize at first how hard the ground was, and that despite my efforts I was making scarcely any progress. But after a while I abandoned the shovel and found something more efficient: a pointed metal bar that was lying in a heap of other bits and pieces. I pressed it into service as a pick.

After a time my arms began to ache and I could feel blisters forming on the palms of my hands. I was drenched with sweat; it was running into my eyes and down my chin. But I carried on with my revolting task. I had to be sure.

Suddenly a terrible stench arose, so strong it made me sway on my feet. I backed away giddily and vomited.

When the spasms were over I steeled myself to start digging again. One last effort! I was almost there! The end of my pick was beginning to unearth foul insects, but also fragments of paper, the kind used for drawings and diagrams.

And then the body appeared.

Not all of it. Putrefied flesh and rotten clothing had mingled into a formless, indescribable mass. There was an arm . . . a dreadfully damaged hand . . . And on the wrist – absurd detail – a watch.

But it wasn't Yolande.

It was a man I'd never seen before. At least I didn't think so. It was hard to be sure. The head was enclosed in a horrible cowl of clay, and I couldn't bring myself to remove it to expose the face. There couldn't have been much of that left, anyway. He'd been there for several months.

I stood for ages staring idiotically into the hole, until I was seized with nausea again. That brought me back to reality. There was no point in hanging around – I'd seen all there was to see here. There was thinking to be done, but that could wait until I got home. I put my jacket and overcoat back on, wiped down all the surfaces my fingers might have touched, and opened the door.

When I got outside, the skinny dog rushed at me from behind a pile of rubbish, and this gave me an idea. I grabbed the hound by the scruff of the neck – it was a good sort and didn't put up any resistance – dragged it over to the workshop, pushed it through the door and shut it in.

Whatever next?

9 *Hélène's theory*

I got back home and took two baths to get rid of the
smell of death that seemed to permeate my whole body.
I had no appetite after my macabre discovery, so I
called Régine instead. I could tell from her voice she
still hadn't got over the night before. I asked her
whether Yolande had come back. She hadn't, so Rita
had called the police. It was obviously the best thing
to do. I hung up, lit my pipe, and made my way, in
no particular hurry, to the agency.

'Well,' said Hélène with a smile. 'This is a jolly good
place to work. You hardly ever see the boss.'

I sat down. 'Would you rather I was always undoing
your apron strings?' I asked.

She blushed. That's one of the things I like about
her.

'No smutty jokes, if you don't mind,' she said. 'What
have you been doing since the day before yesterday?'

'Plenty!'

'Have you managed to dig up that model from
P.P.T.?'

It wasn't the verb I'd have chosen.

I told Hélène I'd found the model, then lost her
again.

'Well, well, well,' she said. She sniffed. 'Is that her perfume?'

'No. I've been soaking myself in eau de cologne.'

'To disinfect yourself?'

'Yes,' I said. 'I'd just got back from the Grande-Jatte. A charming place. Full of surprises.'

I told her what had surprised me.

'My God!' she exclaimed in horror. 'Who do you think—'

'A friend of Désiris's,' I said. 'Désiris must have bumped him off before doing in his wife and shooting himself.'

'Her lover?'

'I don't think so,' I said. 'It's more likely to have had something to do with that invention everyone's so worked up about. The bits of paper in the earth round the body are the kind that's used by draughtsmen. Viénot must be right, and Marc must be wrong. Désiris hadn't run out of ideas. He'd finished his design, but held back some key factors without which the drawings were incomprehensible. Maybe he'd hidden them in the workshop, and the other bloke came looking for them, either to destroy them or to exploit them himself. Désiris found him, there was a fight, and the other man was accidentally killed. Or else he'd already destroyed the papers and Désiris killed him intentionally. At first he didn't panic too much. Just buried the body, not very deep. But later on it all started to prey on his mind – the loss of drawings he couldn't reproduce; the murder . . . It could have driven him out of his mind. Mark you, I'm only guessing. The cops will tell us more – about the body, at any rate.'

'Have you told them?'

'I left it to a stray dog that I shut in the workshop. It must be kicking up a hell of a row by now. Someone's bound to go and have a look, even in that godforsaken hole. They'll let the dog out, and then they'll see the rest.'

'But what have Yolande's kidnappers got to do with all this?' said Hélène. 'Are they interested in the invention, as well as Viénot?'

'They certainly are,' I said.

'Are they friends of Désiris's, too?'

'I don't know,' I said. 'They took Yolande to the island, and they know where the workshop is. But that doesn't prove anything.'

'And what about Yolande herself?'

'I tried to be clever about her, like Viénot, and look where it got me. I could kick myself for not trying to stop the kidnappers in the rue du Dobropol. Still, what's done is done, damn it! I can't go back on it now. If only I knew what those bastards looked like.'

'Didn't you see them?' said Hélène.

'Oh, yes,' I said. 'I know they were armed, and wearing coats and hats, and one of them had something on that caught the light – probably a wristwatch. Fat lot of use that is!'

'No point in moaning,' she said. 'You wouldn't be any better off if you knew exactly what they looked like. And how would it change the girl's situation? No, the police know she's disappeared, even if they don't know about the kidnapping, so the only thing to do is wait till they come up with something.'

Wise words. But I couldn't wait. I shook my head. 'No,' I said, clenching my fists. 'You're right – there's no point in it, but I must try to find out who they are.

Then I won't just feel I've abandoned the poor girl.'

'It's up to you,' she said. 'Who are you going to find out from – Dany Darnys?'

'Her!' I said. 'All she could say was that they looked like thugs! She can't help. But there *is* old Huguette de Mèneval – the Countess. The two men went to her place, too, which makes me think they know Yolande better than Viénot does. They knew she lived in the rue Rochefort, *and* that she has a scar on her thigh.'

Hélène frowned. ' "Looked like thugs," ' she said slowly, as though she'd put her finger on some vital detail. In fact she was merely running it down the bridge of her charming nose. 'Did anyone ever find out where Désiris got the money from to set himself up on the Ile de la Grande-Jatte?'

'They didn't try,' I said. 'It wasn't that important. All the police had to do was record that there'd been a murder and a suicide, and go on to something else. Which is what Faroux did.'

'But Madame Désiris was suspicious about where the money came from,' said Hélène, 'and she hired you to find out.'

'Steady, sweetie,' I said. 'That was just a pretext. Désiris hadn't only just got hold of the money. He'd been on the island for months.'

'Since when exactly?'

'I don't know, several months. Good heavens, why are we getting so worked up about the money? Madame Désiris just told me the first story that came into her head. I believe it was her husband's behaviour that was bothering her. If he'd just killed the chap whose body I found this morning. Perhaps even . . . Yes – look. Suppose Madame Désiris got wind of the murder and called me in to find out what had happened, and to protect her. Then Désiris found out and bumped her off, too. But it didn't really solve anything. He'd got two murders to answer for now. So he committed suicide to escape the consequences, taking care to destroy all trace of his invention at the same time. But weren't you just going to offer a suggestion?'

'I wouldn't go as far as that! But I did want to ask a question.'

'Go ahead.'

'What if Désiris and these thugs had done something against the law? Taken part in a hold-up or something?'

'Désiris a gangster?' I said.

'Why not?'

'I suppose anything's possible these days,' I sighed. 'OK – let's suppose he's a gangster as well as an engineer. He and some accomplices rob a bank, say, then he goes calmly back to work on his invention. But it doesn't necessarily follow that his accomplices were the same men as those who attacked Dany, frightened the Countess, and then kidnapped Yolande. And if they were, it doesn't tell us why they did it.'

'Yes, it does,' she said. 'They're looking for something.'

'What?'

'The invention Marc Covet mentioned in his article in the *Crépu*. They've followed the same line of reasoning as Viénot.'

I brandished my pipe in protest. 'No, Hélène. They're not the kind to go after an invention that would only be profitable in the long term, if at all. Money would be a different matter.'

'Why not money, then?'

I don't know whether she'd caught a flea, but as she was speaking she rubbed one leg against the other, making her dress ride above her knee. Perhaps it was just excitement.

'Désiris and some accomplices rob a bank,' she went on. 'The others get caught because they're known crooks. The police don't bother Désiris because the others don't talk, and because he's got a clean record. So he keeps the swag.'

'And now the others are after it – is that it?' I said.

'Why not?'

I started to laugh. 'If the accomplices were let out of prison after just a few months, I'd like to know the name of the nice kind judge that sentenced them! And what's more, Désiris would have had to be the gang leader for the others to have handed over all the money to him. Come, come, my love – that won't wash!'

'All right, make fun of me if you like,' she said, sticking to her guns. 'But just listen . . . Are you listening?'

'Yes.'

'No, you're not. You're looking up my skirt.'

'That doesn't stop me listening,' I said.

'Oh, yes it does,' she said, pulling it down almost to her ankles. It was only a short skirt, but the intention was there. The show was over.

'You don't seem very quick-witted today,' she continued. 'You haven't been coshed too, have you?'

'Not yet,' I said. 'Perhaps that's the trouble.'

'Or perhaps Régine tired you out. Or was it Yolande, or Rita?'

'Why should you think that?' I said.

'With intellectuals like them anything can happen,'

she replied. 'Anyway, as I was saying, the accomplices might have been arrested for some other reason than robbery. And they might have escaped. It happens. And if they entrusted the money to Désiris, it wasn't because he was the ringleader, but precisely because he wasn't a professional gangster, and they knew that if anything went wrong the police would never suspect him of having it.'

'Maybe,' I said with a yawn. 'I won't argue. I've rather lost interest in this conversation.'

'I don't see why.'

'I don't see Y, either,' I said. 'I see Z. Z for zero!'

'Idiot!' she said.

We didn't speak for a while. Hélène was sulking. I was weighing up her theory. It was crazy. It didn't seem to me to hold water. And yet . . . You never can tell. I tapped out my pipe and filled it again.

'Let's each follow our own hunch,' I said. 'It'll make us think we're doing something useful. I'm going to ask the Countess a few questions. You . . . Wait a minute!'

I looked up the number of the Dugat factory in Levallois, then called it, pretending I was a copper. I got the information I was after: Désiris had left the firm at the end of April 1957: he'd taken his holidays early and then extended them without letting his employers know.

'When did his holidays start?' I asked.

'11 February.'

'Do you know where he went?'

'No, superintendent. He didn't send any postcards. When his official holiday was over we wrote to him in the rue Alphonse-de-Neuville saying how surprised we were that he hadn't come back. But he was still away, and hadn't left any forwarding address. Then, when we phoned, we got Madame Désiris, and she didn't know where he was, either.'

'Thank you, monsieur,' I said.

'At your service. Is there something new on the suicide?'

'No, no. We're just tying up a few loose ends.'

I hung up, and so did Hélène. She'd been listening on the extension.

'From the middle of February to the end of April 1957 . , .' I said. 'Hélène, I'd like you to go the National Library and look up the newspapers covering that period. Take down details of all the crimes committed in Paris and elsewhere – Désiris must have been away from Paris for those two and a half months – and the names of everyone arrested or suspected. Anything, in short, that might support your theory. After all, it was *your* idea! I don't think it'll get us very far, but it'll help pass the time. I'm off to see Madame Huguette de Mèneval.'

10 *The aristocracy of the boudoir*

The house in the rue Rochefort where the old courtesan was living out the last stage of a hedonistic and lucrative existence was quite different from the Désiris residence in the rue Alphonse-de-Neuville. More elegant, more ritzy, much more prosperous-looking. And it was set back from the street by a garden with a couple of trees in it. It was built on three floors; the top one was an artist's studio.

There was a large carriage entrance opening on to the street, with an artist's palette and brushes carved over it; a constant stream of carriages and cabs must have passed in and out in its owner's heyday. A small door for pedestrians had been let into one half of the huge double gate.

I pulled the brass chain hanging down by the door-post, and a bell jangled somewhere inside the house. Footsteps crunched on gravel. An old woman came and opened the small door. She was a typical 'help', not at all like the standard image of a courtesan's soubrette, ready to lend a hand or a leg when things got busy. Admittedly Madame Mèneval now lived in retirement. I gave the old girl my card, and without more ado she showed me into a drawing-room on the ground floor, furnished with an ill-assorted collection of furniture and pictures, a grand piano and a harp.

It seems Sarah Bernhardt used to live in a complete shambles – a combination of oriental bazaar and flea market. Perhaps ladies aspiring to share her notoriety, even by means of very different talents, thought they had to do the same.

While the elderly servant went to tell her mistress I was there, I examined a painting hanging in the place of honour. It showed a smiling young woman with a sumptuous *décolleté*, a body that could have raised the dead, and an expression that plainly said 'Come up and see me some time!' A gilt plaque on the frame informed the connoisseur that this was a portrait of Mademoiselle de Mèneval, painted by Archet in 1908 and exhibited in the Salon the same year.

From behind me came a sound like the clicking of bones, and I turned to see a drape drawn aside in a corner of the room and the hostess come in, the ghost of the woman in the picture.

Régine had said she must be about eighty, and she looked it. I searched that gaunt frame in vain for vestiges of past beauty. She had been so generous with her charms there were none left. She was dressed in a style that jumbled together the fashions of her own youth and those of the present day. The result was depressing: she looked like a fortune-teller, which was how Régine and the other girls actually saw her. Her hair was bleached, and although her eyes were still bright, her heavy make-up couldn't disguise the dark rings underneath them. Those rings weren't anything new, but whereas in the old days they'd been the result of nights of pleasure, they were now only the sign of a tired heart. Not that it had ever been involved in the parodies of love which were all she'd ever known. But hearts can be worn out through lack of use. Her legs weren't in any better condition, and she crept towards me leaning on a stick. It was the stick that had caused the clicking I'd noticed earlier, though that funereal rattle was reinforced by the jangle of numerous bracelets, and by the four strings of pearls that festooned a mercifully modest neckline. Even so, the cracking of stubborn joints must have made up quite a part of the sinister chorus.

She had my card in her hand, and when she spoke she sounded both worried and curious.

'You are Monsieur Nestor Burma?'

What a voice! Fifty years ago, what with the smile and the 'come hither' look in the picture, this place must have been Heartbreak House. I bowed.

'At your service, Madame la comtesse,' I said.

She was pleased by my using the title, and told me to be seated.

'I see from your card,' she said, 'that you are a private detective. How *can* you be of service to me?'

'I can't,' I said. 'It's you, madame, who can be of use to me. Among other things, I'm looking for information about two previous tenants of yours: Charles Désiris and Yolande Mège.'

On the way to her house I'd decided not to beat about the bush. I knew she was interested in money, and I had a plan. I produced a wad of notes from my pocket, not quite knowing what I'd do if she got angry. It must have taken her back to her youth, because she didn't.

'Désiris and Yolande?' she said.

'Yes.'

'Why?'

'Madame,' I said, smiling, 'a private detective's most important virtue is discretion.'

What I meant was that I wouldn't tell her who I was working for, or why, but nor, if she accepted the cash, would I split about that. She got the message.

'What do you want to know?' she said in a voice she must have used years ago when she said 'Yes' to a suitor. And quite naturally, as though she wasn't even aware of it, her hand came to rest palm upwards on her knee. All I had to do was put the wad in it. I did so.

'Everything you know yourself, madame,' I said.

We then had what sounded almost like a society chat.

But in the midst of her protestations about how fond she was of the young ladies from the rue de Dobropol, whom she thought of almost as daughters, I learned that, shortly before his 'fatal decision', Désiris had been behaving strangely.

'How do you mean?' I asked.

'Well,' she said, 'Désiris was usually very gentle, kind and considerate. But that day, for some reason or other, he completely lost his temper. He was absolutely fuming, apparently . . .'

' "Apparently?" Weren't you actually there?' I said.

'No. I was out, and only found out about it when I got home. He'd calmed down somewhat by then, but he was still furious. The way he looked at me! Yolande didn't say anything, but I think he must have assaulted her. At any rate, he'd thrown one of my curios across the room – luckily not one I was particularly attached to – and it smashed against a picture.'

I turned to the portrait.

'No, not that one,' she said quickly. 'Thank God, not that one! One of the pictures upstairs, fortunately. But still, I wasn't very pleased. It's quite valuable – a self-portrait by Frédéric Langlat. Perhaps you've heard of him?'

'No,' I said.

'It was he who had this house built. Then Baron Eustache bought it, and later on . . .'

'It came to you?'

'Yes,' she said with a sigh. 'People really knew how to live in those days.'

I agreed politely, then changed the subject. I could do without a list of her lovers. 'So Désiris lost his temper?' I said.

'Yes.'

'When? Can you remember the date?'

'It was the beginning of March. The second or third.'

'In other words, a few days before he . . .'

'Yes.'

'And how did he behave over the next few days?'

'I don't know,' she said. 'We lived quite independently, you see. They rented the two upper floors, and were quite free to come and go as they wished. There's a separate side entrance from the street into the garden. It leads to an outside staircase that goes directly up to the first floor. So I hardly saw him after that incident. But there were no more rows, and Yolande didn't say anything was wrong. Then . . . well . . . he . . .'

'Killed himself,' I said.

We observed a minute's silence.

'Think back, Madame la comtesse,' I said at last. 'Was that the only time Désiris acted strangely?'

'Yes,' she said.

I rustled a few thousand-franc notes in my pocket, and thought I saw her ears prick up under those lustreless locks. She could still hear all right.

'Well, there was the business of the underclothes,' she ventured. 'But I don't think that can be of any importance.'

'Tell me anyway,' I said. 'I'm very interested in underclothes.'

'Men's underclothes.'

'Oh . . . But tell me all the same.'

'It was my maid who found them. Just a few days after Monsieur Charles had got so angry. Of course, it was too late to ask him for an explanation . . . But such a waste of two brand-new shirts, using them as rags! Most peculiar. But as I said, it was too late to go into it, because he'd just . . . I didn't breathe a word about it to Yolande, of course. She was so upset.'

'Yes, yes,' I said, 'but what exactly was it your maid found?'

'Two shirts in among the dirty linen, with stains on them that looked like blood.'

I didn't let on, but I was beginning to get suspicious. The Countess was giving me too much for my money.

'Blood?' I said.

'Yes. As if he'd used the shirts to wipe up blood.'

'Come, come,' I said. 'Could Désiris have murdered someone here in this house without you and Yolande knowing about it?'

'What on earth can you mean, monsieur?' she said angrily.

'I don't mean anything,' I said. 'You say "blood", I say "murder". It's quite logical.'

'But it's impossible!'

'So much the better,' I said.

I ran my hand along my trouser leg, smoothing out the bank notes in my pocket. She wasn't getting any more of them out of me now.

'What's more,' I said, 'it's very difficult to get rid of a body. You'd be bound to have stumbled on it by now.'

'Please!' she said. She fluttered her hand at me and fidgeted about on her chair. Her bracelets did a sort of *danse macabre*.

'I'm sorry,' I said.

I changed the subject and started to talk about Yolande. The old girl was amazed I knew so much about her. I told her how I'd introduced Yolande to her 'double', Dany Darnys.

'Yolande always wanted to act!' exclaimed the Countess.

'Well, now's her chance!' I said, wincing at the thought of the night before.

'She told me she was going into the movies when she left here in April. They all want to break into films!' said the old woman.

She laughed, and her voice cracked. It was nothing like as attractive as her speaking voice.

'Tell me,' she chortled. 'Rita's worried about Yolande, but there's no need, is there? You're looking after her, aren't you?'

'Not in the way you mean,' I said.

She stopped laughing. 'Oh, I thought . . .'

'I just introduced her to Mademoiselle Darnys and left them together. Rita's the girl Yolande's staying with, isn't she? What's she worried about?'

'Yolande didn't go back there last night, and Rita

called me this morning to ask me if I'd seen her. Naturally I said I hadn't. But . . .' she gave me an appraising look '. . . I just thought, to look at you, that it would have been quite natural.'

'Thanks for the compliment,' I laughed. 'But no. I left Yolande with Mademoiselle Darnys. They must have taken to one another, and she stayed the night. That's quite natural, too.'

'Yes, of course.'

'So don't worry about her,' I said. 'But, while we're on the subject of Yolande, I was told two men came here looking for her while she was away. Did you know them?'

'Good heavens, no!' she protested.

'Tell me what they looked like, then,' I said, 'unless they paid you to keep quiet. And even if they did, no one will know it was you who told me.'

I slipped out a few notes, the one-time temptress let herself be tempted again, and after a bit of shilly-shallying gave me a description of her unwelcome visitors. One was tall, the other short . . . My money had been wasted. What did I expect? Would I ever learn? 'When did they come?' I asked.

'In October.'

The same time as Dany Darnys had had a similar visit.

'Did they threaten you?'

'No. But they weren't friendly. I was frightened.'

'Were you alone?' I said.

'Yes. The maid was out.'

'What did they ask you, exactly?'

'They wanted Yolande's address. But I couldn't give it to them because I didn't know it.'

'One tall and one short you say?'

'Yes.'

Laurel and Hardy, thought I. So they weren't anything like the two men who'd kidnapped Yolande. I hadn't got much of a look at *them* but they'd both seemed about the same height – a little above the average. Anyway, I made a mental note of what the Countess had said.

'Right,' I said. 'Thank you, madame. That will be all. I'm sorry to have bothered you.'

I stood up and she followed suit.

'Just one more thing before I go,' I said. 'Would you mind if I had a look round the rooms you let to Désiris?'

'That's what the others wanted to do,' she said.

'Did you let them?' I asked.

She said she had.

'And what did they do up there?' I said. Then, remembering the state of her legs: 'But perhaps you didn't go with them?'

'Yes, I did,' she said. 'But they didn't do anything. Just had a look round and then left.'

'And that's all I'll do,' I said. 'Would you be kind enough to take me up?'

We went up a polished oak staircase to the first floor. In contrast to the clutter downstairs, the apartment here was comfortably but very sparsely furnished – my hostess explained that a lot of things had been moved downstairs. She pointed out the damage – since repaired – that Désiris had done to the picture when he shied a vase at it. The canvas in question depicted Frédéric Langlat, an intense-looking cove with a beard, getting ready to dash off this, his own self-portrait. It might have been valuable. Anything is possible. The walls were covered with a rather unpleasant reddish tapestry.

We went out of this room, which was directly underneath the studio on the third floor, and into a bedroom with a staircase in one corner. Another climb, and we were in the very place where the conscientious dauber had produced his masterpiece. It had been tastefully transformed into a small flat.

Then we went down to the ground floor again. 'The only place you could hide something up there would be in a drawer,' I said.

'Hide something?' she said with surprise.

'Yes,' I said. 'Do you know what the men were looking for?'

'No,' she said. 'Do you?'

'I'm not sure. Dough, probably. Désiris must have had a packet.' (Thanks for the tip, Hélène!)

'Dough?' echoed the countess.

'Money,' I said.

'I understand the word,' she said. 'It's the idea that surprises me.'

'Me too,' I said.

'Where could he have hidden it?'

'Ah! That is the question!' I said. 'Not upstairs, at any rate. Too bare. Possibly down here.' I gestured towards all the bric-à-brac. 'Well, dear madame, this time I really am going.'

'Julie will show you out,' she said, tugging at a bell-pull. 'Au revoir, Monsieur Burma.'

'Au revoir, Countess,' I said, and kissed her hand.

On the way out I winked at the delightful creature in the portrait. She'd wound all the men round her little finger, in her day. Now the flesh might be weak, but the spirit was still willing. Ah, well. We all have to do the best we can.

Outside, as the old retainer led me through the dreary little garden towards the gate, I suddenly heard through the gathering dusk the exquisite trill of a harp.

Wrong again, Burma . . . I'd imagined the old girl already turning the place upside down, looking for the money.

I crossed the street, got back in my car and made for the office. On the way I stopped in a bar and rang Roger Zavatter. In another bar.

'Now someone else is trying to lead me up the garden path,' I said.

'How unkind,' he said. 'But what do you want *me* to do?'

'The same as you did with Viénot,' I said. 'Tail them.'

'OK. Who is it?'

'Huguette de Mèneval.'

He whistled. 'What a name to go to bed with!'

'Not any more,' I said. 'She's eighty and walks with a stick.'

'Damn!' he said.

I gave him the address and some other particulars, then hung up.

When I got back to the office, I just had time to register the fact that Hélène was still at the Library and hadn't even left me a note, when the doorbell rang.

I found two coppers wiping their feet on the mat. One of them was Fabre, Faroux's assistant.

'Lucky there's a nice warm café across the road,' he said. 'We've been waiting for you for ages. The super wants to see you.'

'What about?' I said.

'He didn't say.'

I went quietly. Fairly quietly.

11 *The killers of the rue du Dobropol*

Florimond stood up when I came in.

'Sit down,' he said, dropping back into his seat. As he did so he brushed against the shade of his desk-lamp in such a way that the light hit me right between the eyes, while the upper part of his own face was left in shadow. Standard Faroux practice.

'What's up?' I said.

By way of reply he tapped a file that lay open in front of him, and cleared his throat. 'This has come in from my friends in the missing persons department,' he said. 'Yolande Mège, artiste, missing since yesterday. Shared a flat with a girl called Marguerite Marson in the rue du Dobropol. It was she who reported the disappearance. Inquiries have been made on the basis of what she said. It seems someone came to the flat last night, looking for Mademoiselle Mège. Mademoiselle Marson wouldn't open up, so the bloke slipped his card under the door. His name's Marcel Viénot. He went back to the flat early this morning, and he's been questioned. Do you know what he said in his statement?'

'That he got Yolande Mège's address from Dany Darnys, who'd got it from Nestor Burma,' I said.

'Exactly,' said Faroux. 'Now that *is* a surprise!'

'What?'

'You coming across right away. Is this a new tactic?'

'It's not a tactic at all,' I said. 'I've nothing against telling you the truth . . . when I don't have any choice.'

'Very funny,' he said. 'The missing persons department would like to hear that. It would confirm their opinion of you. They alerted me as soon as your name came up.'

'How kind,' I said.

'On the contrary,' he said. 'They're hoping that one day you'll go too far, get into real trouble, and pull me down with you.'

'Nice friends you have,' I said.

He rolled a cigarette; lit it. A cloud of smoke started climbing towards the ceiling. 'And there's another thing,' he went on. 'Marcel Viénot works in the motor-car business, just as Charles Désiris did. You remember him?'

'Very well,' I said. 'The bloke who turned up his toes.'

'Yes. Like a lot of people who have anything to do with you.'

'You don't think it's me who kills them, do you?'

'The idea has crossed my mind,' he said. 'And there's a third thing: Viénot's come clean. He's told us why he was interested in Yolande Mège.'

'Because she was Désiris's mistress. Isn't that it?'

'Exactly. And you knew.'

'So what?' I said. 'No one could have been more surprised than I was when I found out. But that wasn't why *I* was interested in Yolande. I spent several hours with her before I took her round to see Dany Darnys, and Désiris's name never so much as crossed my lips. You can ask her when you find her.'

'*If* we find her,' said Faroux. 'I'm afraid she may be yet another dame who's bought it through getting to know you.'

'What do you mean?'

'Right,' he said, taking a sheet of paper out of the file. 'Tell me why you're so interested in this Yolande Mège.'

'I'm not,' I said. 'I *was* interested on behalf of Dany Darnys.'

I told him the *Purely Parisian Thrills* story, and as I did so he seemed to refer to the report in front of him.

'Yes,' he said when I'd finished, 'that's what Viénot said. He also said you'd been working for him without realizing it.'

'Quite true,' I said. 'But there's no reason for you to get steamed up.'

'There are several!' he said. 'To begin with, the girl you were interested in has disappeared.'

'That's not my fault,' I said. 'I took her to Dany Darnys's place at eleven o'clock last night, and left them to get on with it. Perhaps she's still there.'

'No. She left at midnight.'

I shrugged. 'What do you expect me to say?'

'Levallois police station had an anonymous phone-call last night, saying there was a car driving around there with two blokes on board who'd been seen molesting a girl. The registration number was – ' he consulted his file ' – 2107 AB 75. The caller must have had pretty good eyesight to get all that. Anyway, a Tallemet with the same plates was found abandoned near a breaker's yard on the outskirts of Clichy this afternoon. Registered under the name of Yolande Mège.'

'Was she in it?' I said.

'No,' he said. 'But that doesn't improve matters.

Look, Burma, I don't like you being mixed up in this.
It's another dirty business.'

How did he think *I* felt? I spent my whole life trying
to avoid complications! But there's nothing you can do
about coincidence, for God's sake!

At last Faroux seemed convinced, and I saw with
relief that he was about to tell me to blow. 'Anyway,'
he said, 'I think I'll take another look at the Désiris
case. Perhaps—'

He was interrupted by the telephone. He picked it
up. Listened for a few seconds. Then stiffened. 'What!
The Grande-Jatte? Wait – I'll take it on another line.'

He got up. 'Good God!' he said. 'I certainly am going
to take another look at the Désiris case!' And he gave
me a really dirty look. 'Stay where you are,' he said,
and rushed out of the room.

I got up and went over to the window. The lights on
the Pont St-Michel and some neon signs on the opposite
bank were reflected in the sombre waters of the Seine.
Through the dull roar of the traffic I seemed to hear the
barking of a dog. A dog that couldn't stand being locked
up any longer with a stinking corpse.

Faroux was back ten minutes later. 'Hop it!' he said,
grabbing his coat off the hook. 'We'll talk again later
if necessary. And it certainly will be.'

'What's up?' I asked.

'Read tomorrow's papers.'

We charged downstairs together, accompanied by his
escort of coppers. When we got outside they shed me,
crammed themselves into a car, and went tearing off,
no doubt in the direction of the Grande-Jatte.

'So there we are, Hélène,' I said, rattling the ice in
my glass of vermouth. 'How did *you* get on?'

'No luck,' she said. 'There weren't any major robberies between 15 February and 30 April 1957. All the gangsters must have been on holiday.' She shook her head. 'It was a crazy idea.'

'What did I tell you?' I said. 'Mind you, it was worth a try. But a hold-up wasn't the only way Désiris could have got hold of money illegally. It's more likely he made use of his professional skills. It's a thought . . . But I'm not going to waste time following it up now. I'm sure it wouldn't help, given the present developments.'

'Perhaps not.'

She drained her glass and looked at her watch. 'My word! Almost nine. This feels like overtime.' She got up. 'Need me any more?'

'No.'

I helped her on with her coat.

'Are you staying on?'

'Just for a bit,' I said.

'Good night.'

'Good night, Hélène.'

The sound of her high heels receded down the stairs.

I tried to think, but without much success, so I decided to give it a rest and called Régine.

'Could I come round and see you?'

'Yes. If you like.'

She didn't sound very enthusiastic. She sounded scared.

'Have you had dinner?' I said.

'I'm not hungry.'

'I thought maybe you'd be thirsty,' I said, unwrapping the bottles I'd bought on the way.

'Oh, you shouldn't have!' said Régine absently. She seemed tense, and perhaps a little put out at seeing me.

I'd noticed when she opened the door that her dressing-gown was as firmly shut as the tax-inspector's mouth when you ask for a few months' grace. Now it had worked open a little, and I glimpsed some green underwear, with lace at strategic points. But neither of us was in the mood. Something was wrong. She was as taut as a violin string, and her hair was dishevelled.

'I hope I'm not disturbing you,' I said.

'It depends what you mean by "disturbing",' she said ungraciously.

I shrugged. 'Not what you seem to think,' I said. 'I wondered if I'd woken you up.'

I grabbed a whisky bottle and started struggling with the top.

'At just after nine?' she said wryly.

'Being tired's like being hungry,' I said. 'It can happen at any time.'

'Well, I'm not tired,' she said.

'Or hungry,' I said.

'I was watching the telly.'

'Something good?'

'I didn't notice.'

She nodded toward the bottles.

'That was a good idea, though,' she said. 'The cellar's bare.'

'Look,' I ventured, 'I don't want to be a nuisance, but it's obvious something's wrong.'

I put the whisky down and took her gently by the shoulders.

'What's the trouble?' I said. 'Tell me about it. I can take it.'

She shuddered, then pulled away. 'It's nothing,' she said. 'Really.'

But she wouldn't look me in the face.

'You're frightened,' I said.

By way of reply, she fell into my arms and began to cry. It was lucky I'd got rid of the bottle. The scent of her perfume wafted up as her hair brushed against my face. But something else, too, sensual and warm. I could feel her heart beating, and mine echoing it. Her bosom heaved under her flimsy nylon nightdress. But what she needed wasn't love. It was something else – something to calm her down.

'Oh, Nes,' she whispered between racking sobs. 'I *am* frightened – yes.'

'What of?'

'Of what's going on.'

'Nothing else?'

'Isn't that enough?' she said. 'Poor Yolande.'

'We'll find her,' I said.

'You're only saying that to reassure me.'

'Just calm down.'

I ran my fingers through the warmth of her hair and stroked her neck. Gradually she relaxed and stopped crying. Then I took her by the chin and tilted her face up towards me. There was something in her tearful expression that she couldn't put into words.

I led her over to the sofa, sat her down and gave her a handkerchief.

'Blow your nose,' I said, 'and say "thank you" to the nice gentleman who's going to fix a snort for the prettiest drunk in the XVIIth arrondissement.'

I went and mixed two whiskies. She downed hers in one gulp.

'Still,' she murmured, shaking her head. 'Poor Yolande.'

'Is that what's upsetting you so?' I said.

'Isn't it natural? I've been imagining terrible things ever since yesterday. I haven't been able to eat or sleep.'

'Only drink,' I said.

'Yes, but it didn't do me any good,' she said. 'I couldn't get really drunk.'

'It's always the way,' I said. 'We almost never get anywhere by trying. And yet sometimes good things come right out of the blue.'

Bad things too, I thought.

But I just said: 'Have a drop more whisky and stop worrying. We'll find Yolande. The cops are on to it now.'

'They've been crawling over the house all day.'

'Did they question you?'

'They questioned almost everyone.'

I took her hand in both mine, and held it tight.

'You didn't say anything, did you?' I said.

She shivered. 'Just what we agreed,' she said. 'That we left her at Dany Darnys's place.'

'Good girl,' I said. 'You've really got nothing to—'

I stopped, and began to laugh. Régine looked at me in astonishment.

'What's so funny?' she said.

'Just the way I talk to you. Sometimes I speak as if I hardly know you; sometimes as if we've known each other for ever. Haven't you noticed? I must be going ga-ga!'

It was her turn to take my hand in hers.

'Perhaps you'd like to know me better,' she whispered,

with an eloquent sideways glace through her long lashes. 'Sometimes these things just happen . . .'

And before I knew what had hit me I was lying underneath her on the divan. Her breath came in gasps, her heart was thumping against mine, our lips met.

But it was all too precise, too calculated. There wasn't the same spontaneity as before. I could feel the difference: it was compensation for something. Something she hadn't dared tell me. She felt guilty about it, and giving herself to me was her way of trying to ease her conscience.

'Nes . . . Nes . . .' she murmured.

And then I knew. She'd told the police about the kidnapping. But Faroux hadn't mentioned that he knew about it, and knew that I did too: he was holding it back, giving me plenty of rope to hang myself. But Régine wasn't used to being mixed up in violence. She'd cracked, and didn't dare tell me so. That's what was torturing her. Ah, well. Too bad! I didn't hold it against her. I wasn't even going to let on that I'd twigged.

'Nes . . .' she whispered. 'Nes . . .'

The silence was broken by the sound of an approaching car. It stopped in the street below and a door slammed loudly. Then we heard the dull hum of the lift ascending, followed a few minutes later by a clatter of high heels right over our heads.

'She makes enough racket,' I said.

'It's Consuelo,' Régine said. 'I think she goes to bed with those heels on.'

'Is she the Spanish girl?'

'Yes.'

She obviously wasn't Swedish, was she? I wondered

why I'd asked such a stupid question. There was something about the name that had triggered a vague memory. I took a slug of my whisky to brush away the cobwebs.

'Consuelo . . .' I muttered.

'Can't you stop talking about her?' said Régine, digging me in the ribs.

'It's not what you think,' I said.

The high heels were clacking about again upstairs. In my brain as well. 'Consuelo Mogador,' I muttered.

And suddenly it came back to me. 'She knew Désiris, didn't she?'

'Please don't talk about that business any more,' Régine begged.

Her voice was no longer blurred by alcohol. It was charged with emotion.

'No, it wasn't her,' I said. 'It was her boyfriend. He and Désiris were buddies. That's what you told me, wasn't it?'

'Yes!' she snapped. 'Now could we change the subject?'

'You know what it's like when you've got something hovering at the back of your mind, don't you?' I urged.

I couldn't tell whether she'd understood the hint, but she didn't say a word. Just looked at me reproachfully.

'I've a good mind to take advantage of being here and go and ask Mademoiselle Mogador some questions before she goes to bed,' I said.

'You must be mad!' cried Régine, clutching my arm so hard I could feel her fingernails. It was getting to be a habit.

'What's all this?' I asked her. 'Are you frightened again?'

'You know I'm frightened all the time,' she said. 'I've told you why I can't take any more.'

'Anyone would think you wanted to stop me seeing the woman upstairs.'

'What? Me?' She gave a strange laugh which was really more like a sob. 'Want to stop you seeing her? Go and see her – go to bed with her if you like!'

She went over and poured herself another whisky with a trembling hand. I picked up the telephone. Upstairs Consuelo was still trotting about. The sound of her heels stopped as soon as the phone rang, but she didn't answer it straight away. At last there came a deafening 'Hello'.

'Hello,' I said. 'Mademoiselle Mogador?'

'Who's speaking?'

She had a strong accent, and she too sounded tense. What was the matter with all these women?

'I'm sorry to disturb you—' I began.

'Who is this?' she interrupted curtly. No nonsense about politeness.

'Nestor Burma. I'm a private detective.'

'*Qué?*'

I repeated it.

'Listen – is this some kind of joke?'

'Not at all,' I said. 'I'd like to see you.'

'At this time of night?'

'*Sí, señorita.*'

'This must be a joke.'

'Not at all,' I said. 'On the contrary, it's *mucho serioso.*'

She didn't answer. She seemed to have gone away. Doubtless to throw up at my awful Spanish . . . But no.

'Private detective did you say?'

'Yes.'

'What do you want to see me about?'

'Several things.'

'It must be a *treek*. Where are you calling from?'

'I'm standing almost next to you. I'm down in Régine Monteuil's flat.'

That gave her something to think about.

'No!'

'Sí!'

'Well, tell Régine to come up with you, then. But I still say it's a *treek*.'

We both hung up. I grabbed a bottle from the table.

'She says she wants you to come up with me,' I said. 'It's not a bad idea. You can do the introduction and break the ice.'

Régine shrugged. 'You *are* crazy,' she grumbled.

But she drew her dressing gown around her more tightly, and we went upstairs. Consuelo was still obviously under the impression it was a trick, and Régine had to say she was there before our hostess would open the door.

'Mother of God!' Consuelo exclaimed when she saw us. 'It was true after all. Come in, *amigos*.'

We followed her pleasing posterior and clicking heels down a hall and into a living-room furnished any old how, where she swung round to face us. Her red gipsy skirt clung to her shapely legs for a second before settling back into its folds. The windows and curtains were closed, and there was a heady scent of perfume.

'Here are my credentials,' I said with a smile, setting down the bottle and holding out my card. Her dark eyes gave me a searching look. 'I wouldn't want you to think I was bluffing,' I explained.

She took the card. 'So it's true!' she said. 'You *are*

a detective. Oh! How amusing!' and she burst into a laugh.

'Pedro!' she called.

A man came out of the next-door bedroom pulling on his jacket. He was about thirty-five, slightly above average height, bronzed and athletic. He was wearing an expensive suit, glasses with tortoise-shell frames, and crêpe-soled shoes. He looked half sportsman, half prosperous business man.

'Look,' said Consuelo, still smiling and passing him my card. 'May I introduce *el señor* Burma, the detective who called up just now.'

'Yes, yes,' he said, glancing at my card and then looking round. 'Hello, Régine.'

'Hello, Monsieur Pierre,' answered Régine shyly.

Monsieur Pierre then came towards me with hand outstretched and an enormous grin. It didn't take much to keep this couple happy. Or so it seemed.

'Delighted to meet you,' I said.

'Fancy calling on people at this hour!' he exclaimed. 'What a joker! But I adore jokers.'

And he laughed to prove it. But he overdid it. He wasn't really a bit amused at my intrusion, and I thought I knew why.

'I'm very sorry to disturb you,' I said, but he waved his hand.

'Not at all,' he said. 'You're not disturbing me in the least. You wanted to talk to Mademoiselle Mogador about something, didn't you?'

'Well . . .' I began.

'I understand,' he said with another false guffaw. 'If you'd known I was here, perhaps . . .'

'. . . perhaps I'd have been even more insistent.'

'Really?' His eyes glinted behind his glasses.

'Yes, really,' I said. 'I brought a bottle. Perhaps we could have a drink.'

'Good idea,' he said. 'Consuelo, would you go and get some glasses? Make yourselves comfortable, my friends!'

We all sat down. Régine didn't seem to be enjoying herself much. She was all hunched up in her dressing-gown. Consuelo fetched a tray of glasses while Monsieur Pierre opened the bottle, then he did the honours.

When we each had a drink in our hand, he said very seriously: 'Go ahead, then. I'm curious to know what you want to see me for.'

'I want some information about a chap whose body I found,' I said.

'What?' he said with a start. Consuelo let out an exclamation in Spanish.

I was rather amused. And they called *me* a joker! 'A chap called Désiris,' I continued. 'An engineer who killed himself on 7 March, after first bumping off his wife. It was I who found them. Nothing extraordinary about that – I specialize in that sort of thing . . . I believe you knew him.'

'Who?'

'Désiris.'

He slowly took a case out of his pocket and extracted a cigarette. 'Désiris?' he said.

'I understand your reluctance to admit you knew him,' I said. 'You never can tell with the police. No one in this house would admit they knew him, after he killed himself. Not even the girl who was his mistress.'

'Look here,' Consuelo cut in, 'we've got nothing to hide, you know.'

'All the more reason to keep quiet,' said Monsieur Pierre philosophically. He put the cigarette case back in his pocket and lit up.

'Yes,' I said. 'But I'm not a cop.'

'Aren't you?' he said. 'What are you, then?'

'A private eye.'

'What's the difference?'

I shrugged. 'You're not being very cooperative, Monsieur . . . Monsieur . . .' I gave him a chance to fill in the name, but he didn't take it.

Instead he gave another laugh: 'What a day!' he said. 'First we have the police on our backs asking questions about Yolande—'

'Désiris's mistress,' I said. He took no notice.

'—and now a private detective working overtime. But very well – ' he made a gesture of resignation ' – I suppose the best way to get rid of you is to tell you all I know. Is that it?'

'Exactly.'

'But I'd like you to tell me what you know, too,' he said. 'Does all this mean Désiris didn't kill himself after all?'

'Oh, he killed himself,' I said, 'but there are a whole lot of ramifications. The only thing I know about your relations with Désiris is what Mademoiselle Monteuil here has told me. It seems you gave a little party here one evening, and that Yolande and Désiris were among the guests. That's how you met, isn't it?'

'I believe so, yes.'

I was about to go on when Régine stood up. She was pale and unsteady. She looked as if she was about to faint.

'I'm . . . I'm leaving,' she managed to get out, running a hand over her forehead. 'I don't feel very well.'

'That'll teach you to go easier on the whisky,' I said.

It wasn't very kind, but she was a bloody nuisance. Getting the bloke to talk at all was like trying to balance the budget, and just as he was beginning to loosen up she had to go and spoil things.

'Has she been drinking?' he said.

'She's upset about Yolande,' I explained.

Monsieur Pierre nodded. Meanwhile Consuelo had hurried to her friend's side. 'Don't go, sweetie,' she said. 'Sit down, and I'll go and get you something to make you feel better.'

Régine sat down again. She really didn't seem well. Consuelo came back from the kitchen with a glass of something effervescent which Régine stoically swallowed. Monsieur Pierre was looking at her anxiously. Probably worried about the parquet floor.

'Feeling better?' Consuelo asked.

'Yes,' said Régine dolefully.

'Go down and put her to bed,' ordered Monsieur Pierre, and Consuelo hauled her off, saying she'd be back in a minute. Monsieur Pierre watched them go thoughtfully. The noise of the front door closing brought him back to earth.

'She can't take her booze,' he observed.

'And gets all worked up about nothing,' I said.

'Very true.' He smiled. 'Where were we?'

'Still talking about Désiris,' I said. 'Did you know each other well?'

'Not at all. We just met and liked one another. I've got dozens of acquaintances like that.'

'How did you meet him?'

'Buying a car from the firm where he worked,' he

said. 'You know what salesmen are like – I always go direct to the factory.'

He was interrupted by the sound of the doorbell. Three little rings. He got up.

'Hell! Why couldn't she have taken her bloody keys!' he said.

Then: 'Stay where you are!'

He was in the hallway before I could move.

I'd been taken aback by the change in his voice, and had got up, unbuttoning my jacket as I did so. I wasn't hot. But the atmosphere had suddenly changed. Something funny was going on.

A confused noise came from the direction of the front door. Before I had time to go and see what was happening, Monsieur Pierre was back. Or rather, backing into the living-room with his hands in the air and two blokes sticking some very unpleasant artillery into his stomach.

There was nothing out of the ordinary about their clothes or physique, and if it hadn't been for their guns you'd have put the complete lack of expression on their faces down to an equivalent lack of brain. As it was they seemed coldly determined, which didn't bode too well.

One of them stepped aside nimbly and took up a position from which he could keep an eye on me. He obviously hadn't expected to find Monsieur Pierre entertaining company, especially company with a gun. He looked a bit surprised, but not too worried about my revolver. He was obviously thinking that with two guns against one, I wasn't likely to try anything. He was right, but I preferred having it in my hand to not having it at all. Especially as I'd been quick enough to find some cover, and was crouching against the wall, behind a wing chair. All we could do was maintain the status quo until such time as one of us did something stupid. It could be a long wait. I only hoped Consuelo would come back and create a diversion.

'Who's this bloke?' my gunman said to Monsieur Pierre without taking his eyes off me. He had a heavy Marseilles accent.

Monsieur Pierre replied from the armchair where he'd been shoved by the second crook, a fellow sporting an elegant cap.

'A cop,' he said, as he sat with both hands on his head, looking down the muzzle of a revolver.

'I was just telling him a lot of rubbish to keep him talking and find out how much he knows, when you went and turned up,' he added contemptuously. 'You don't do things by halves, do you?'

The fellow with the cap gave a nasty laugh.

'What do you expect?' he said. 'We wanted to know how you were getting on. We weren't too happy, you see, about your just dropping us like that. If you did it because you were scared, that means we can't trust you any more. You might talk.'

'Just because someone's scared it doesn't mean he's going to talk,' said Monsieur Pierre. 'I've told you – it just isn't working out. We'll never find it.'

'Rubbish!' said the other. 'You know where the stuff is. You've got the wind up, that's all. The girl must have told you something, and you wanted to have it all to yourself. So you decided to pretend you'd had enough . . . "We'll never do it, lads. We'd better split up. It's been more trouble than it's worth." Like hell!

And we get left like a couple of mugs with less dough than we had when we started, and a lot of other problems into the bargain. While you go off with the lolly and Consuelo. Where is she, by the way?'

'Out to dinner.'

'Oh, yeah? Well, just in case she comes back unannounced . . .' And he went and stood where he could keep an eye on M. Pierre, the door and me. Now they both had me covered, and my gun was about as much use to me as a bra to a dab. What's more, I could feel the first twinges of cramp in my arm.

'So he's a cop, is he?' said the one with the cap.

'Yes,' said M. Pierre. 'The place has been lousy with them all day. Because of the girl.'

'Hey, don't go blaming us for that,' said the Cap. 'And that's another funny thing. Before we picked her up, you told us she knew everything. And I still think she did – that ring she was wearing didn't come out of a Christmas cracker. But when we got her, she claimed she didn't know a thing, and you didn't seem a bit surprised.'

'I'd made a mistake. It can happen to anyone.'

'Not to you. Not any more.'

Monsieur Pierre turned white. He tried to shout, but all that came out was a feeble murmur: 'Look here, you don't mean . . .' The sweat was pouring down his face and his glasses were all steamed up.

'This business about the police is funny, too,' said his former pal deliberately. 'I thought you were stringing them along as protection, because you thought that while they were around we wouldn't dare show our faces. Though that didn't stop us coming to see you as soon as they were gone. All except this one, that is. And he seems quite at home here.'

'We've been had,' grumbled the one from Marseilles. 'Whichever way you slice it, we've been had.'

'Tell me something I don't know!' said the Cap.

'I wasn't going to cut you out,' Monsieur Pierre protested.

'You didn't mind cutting out Sarfotti,' said the one from Marseilles. 'We don't trust you any more.'

'Never mind about that!' roared the Cap. 'We've been had!'

He turned back to Monsieur Pierre. 'So you've made friends with the cops, have you?'

'Let me explain, for God's sake!' said Pierre. 'He's not that kind of cop. He's a private eye – he works for himself.'

'I don't care who he works for,' said the Cap. 'What's he doing here?'

'I think he's looking for the same thing as we are.'

The Cap glared at me balefully. 'Cough up, cop,' he said, 'if that's really what you are.'

My throat felt dry. 'Not any more,' I said.

'What do you mean?'

'I mean I'm not looking any more. Pierre's got the stuff.'

'For God's sake, Paulot, don't listen to him!' Pierre begged.

Then, realizing my accusation was the final nail in his coffin, he threw caution to the winds. He leapt from his chair and rushed towards the Cap, throwing out his arms imploringly as he did so. The Cap, thinking he was being attacked, feinted to the left, ducked to the right, slipped on the polished parquet and fell flat on his face. This created a moment of confusion during which Pierre whipped a pistol from the inside pocket of his jacket. He had nothing to lose. He got off a shot at the Cap, missed him, and was caught by the cross-fire from the two other guns. He pirouetted grotesquely as the impact of the bullets jerked him first to the right and then to the left.

I didn't see any more: the thugs hadn't forgotten me in the excitement, and lead was spitting in my direction, too. As I ducked behind the padded leather back of my wing chair, I heard Pierre go down, bringing the tray with the whisky bottle and glasses crashing to the floor as he did so. I threw myself flat as more bullets thudded into the chair.

Then the firing stopped, and I heard the sound of running feet as the killers made off.

Yet another scrape I'd got out of unscathed! What a laugh! A door slammed. The coast was clear. Come on, Nestor! Up you get. You're not finished yet. I tried to move. It must have been the polish that was keeping me stuck to the floor. It seemed to be oozing between my fingers. Or maybe it was the smell of cordite that was making my head pound. There was a red veil before my eyes. When I closed them, they seemed to slam shut like a door. I knew my eyes felt heavy, but this was ridiculous. Then I heard another door close, high heels, a stifled cry, some oaths.

In this darkness shot through with a million colours, it was too noisy to sleep, so I opened my eyes again. Now the technicolor vision had gone. Everything was a misty red. I thought I saw a pretty leg vanish in the distance. Get up, Nestor. You can think about girls another time. I mustered all my strength, clung on to the chair and somehow pulled myself to a standing position. The room began to spin. Pierre was drifting to and fro between the floor and the ceiling, gliding up and down like an aeroplane, his arms thrown out like wings. Up. Down. He looked like Salvador Dali's Christ. I threw myself down again so the corpse wouldn't land on my head.

'Get out of here,' someone said. It was me.

'Just going,' I answered, polite as ever.

After a brief skiing session I made it along an interminable corridor, then took advantage of the fact that my vision had almost returned to normal to hurl myself against a door with all my might. It wouldn't budge, until my voice reminded me I had to pull. Of course! My right hand felt for the handle, the bolt or whatever, but found nothing. It must have been because it was already holding something. I looked down. There was a revolver gripped between the fingers. My revolver. My fingers. Somehow I managed to get the door open and myself out on to the landing, only to hear what sounded like another shot ring out. But it was merely another door that someone had slammed to when they saw me emerge. Someone else who wanted to get away before the cops turned up. Someone who preferred to keep his visit to Mademoiselle Rita, Madame Coraline, or one of the other adorable creatures a secret, because he'd told his wife he was at a conference in the provinces, or attending an all-night session at the Chamber of Deputies.

I grabbed at the banister, and throwing my weight on it like a sack on a donkey's back, slithered down to the next floor, my feet scarcely touching the stairs.

Régine's key was still in her door. I turned it and went in. She was standing by the window, clinging to the curtains to keep her balance. When she saw me she floated towards me in her transparent night-dress yawning fit to bust her jaw.

Was that the only effect I had on her? We'd see

about that later – and about the things she'd kept from me. For the moment my first priority was to find a wash-basin, fill it with water and plunge my face in it.

'Get out of here,' said my voice again. 'It's not long since it all happened, even if it does seem an age. There wasn't that much noise because they had silencers on their pistols, but people must have noticed it all the same. For their own private reasons, they won't call the police right away. So now's your chance. Get out of here before the house is crawling with cops!'

Then the voice got louder: 'Régine, I've been hit . . . can't walk . . . doctor . . . friend . . . in Neuilly . . . quite near . . . Let's go . . . Stop yawning like that.'

'It's the drink Consuelo gave me,' mumbled Régine.

'Yes . . . Consuelo . . . No need to be afraid any more . . . He's dead . . . We'll go down to your car . . . Before the cops arrive . . . Get your coat on . . . No, like that . . . Don't worry about the rest. Doctor's used to it.'

She was plucky enough to do as I said, and we went down together, she yawning hard, I only half conscious, with my right arm hanging numbly at my side and the gun still heavy in my hand. They were going to have to operate to get it out of my grasp. There was a crack of light showing under the concierge's door, but no one came out to try and stop us, and we got out on to the rue du Dobropol without further incident.

It was freezing, but although I normally hate the cold I could feel it doing me good. I didn't even care that my jacket was open and my tie had disappeared. We climbed into Régine's car, and, yawning still, she pulled away.

Just in time.

We'd only gone a few hundred yards when the silence was shattered by the familiar yowl of a police siren.

I was thrown against the door, sending more waves of pain up to the roots of my hair and down to the soles of my feet. I was bathed in sweat. The car had just hit a pile of sand spilling over from the kerb, and narrowly missed plunging into a tree.

Régine was slumped against the wheel, her head still nodding from the effects of Consuelo's ministrations. I gritted my teeth, took hold of the wheel with my good hand, and did my best to get the car back on the road.

'Régine!' I implored.

She shook her head to clear it, and took the wheel again. And so we zigzagged down the avenue de Neuilly, I pinching her to keep her awake, and the car sending the odd dustbin flying.

Luckily we didn't have very far to go.

12 *Coming round*

'That one didn't have your number on it, either,' said the doctor, with a benevolent smile.

'Thanks, pal,' I said.

I was lying in bed in his spare room. The lamp on the table was giving off a moderate amount of light, but the sky outside the window was ambiguous.

'Is the sun going up or down?' I asked.

'It hasn't been out all day, but theoretically it's going down. It's 4 p.m. on Saturday, 8 November.'

'As bad as that, was it?' I said.

'Not really. You'll be back on your feet by tomorrow. But I wanted you to get some rest, so I gave you some sleeping pills.'

'I suppose that's what's given me this hangover?'

'That and the wound, and the operation, not to mention what you drank before you got here,' said the doctor. 'But it's not for me to criticize.'

'Yes, I had put away quite a few,' I said, 'but I think it was the bullet-hole more than anything. Thanks again, doctor. I'm sorry to have bothered you, but you are the only person I could turn to.'

'You didn't bother me,' he said. 'You were hardly

any trouble. You just passed out into my arms at the door, and I had to carry you into my surgery. The same thing with your friend, which was even more agreeable! But there was nothing seriously wrong with her. She was only drowsy.'

'Drugged,' I said.

'As I found,' said the doctor. 'She should watch herself. One of these days she won't wake up.'

'She didn't know she was taking it,' I said. 'Someone slipped her a Mickey Finn.'

'Oh, I see! That makes much more sense. Anyhow, I put her on the sofa to sleep it off, and she left this morning.'

'Just in her night-dress and fur coat?' I said.

'No. Hélène went and bought her a cheap dress – with your money, I might add.'

'Hélène?' I said.

'Yes. I needed a nurse last night,' he said. 'I hesitated to call her because of – well . . . *you* know – the other girl, especially as she didn't have much on. But someone had to help me, and Hélène was the best person I could think of.'

'Quite right,' I said. 'Is she still here?'

'She's coming back at five o'clock.'

He felt in his pocket and brought out an ugly-looking 7.65 slug. 'This is what we dug out of your bread basket! It might have done a lot more damage. Here – for your collection!'

He put it down on the bedside table, and asked what had led up to my present situation.

So I told him.

'H'm!' he said, pretending to be scandalized. 'No doubt the police would like to hear all that! And here am I operating on you, looking after you, providing you with a hideout, and the police don't know anything about it!'

I shrugged.

'It's in the papers, though,' he added.

'What is?'

'That business in the rue du Dobropol.'

'May I have a look at them,' I said, 'and then perhaps use the phone?'

'Make yourself at home,' he said. 'What more have I got to lose?'

There was an article in *Crépuscule*.

DRAMA IN THE RUE DU DOBROPOL

A mysterious drama took place last night in the rue du Dobropol (XVIIth arrondissement). Unidentified gunmen entered Mlle Consuelo Mogador's flat and shot her friend, M. Pierre Brousse, before making their escape. Mlle Mogador has disappeared. Police are releasing no details concerning the victim. It is worth noting that Mlle Yolande Mège, who disappeared on Thursday, lives in the same building. The police are said to have found significant finger-prints, but are refusing to answer questions about a possible link between the two cases.

I looked to see if there was anything about the Ile de la Grande-Jatte. There was.

WAS CHARLES DESIRIS A MULTI-MURDERER?

A macabre discovery was made yesterday in the workshop of the late Charles Désiris.

The victim has been identified as M. Jean Chambefort, 35, who was employed in the research department of the Dugat Automobile Company, where Désiris also worked until February/March 1957.

An autopsy has revealed that M. Chambefort's death took place nine months ago – i.e., in March, the month when Désiris killed his wife and then committed suicide. The cause of death cannot be ascertained with certainty because the body is an advanced state of decomposition, but foul play is suspected.

In April we suggested that Désiris had taken his own life because he found himself incapable of bringing an invention of his to completion, and that he had killed his wife either in accordance with a suicide pact, or because frustration and resentment had driven him out of his mind.

Today we can add a further reason: Désiris had already killed Jean Chambefort. His motives for doing so are as yet unclear, but fragments of the kind of paper used by draughtsmen and designers were found buried close to Chambefort's body, and there were drawings on them. These are impossible to decipher as the scraps of paper are scorched as well as rotten. It may be that they relate to the uncompleted invention.

Thus it may well be that Charles Désiris killed Chambefort, and then, either out of remorse or from fear of punishment, took his own life.

There followed a few more lines of blather, and then:

Was Chambefort tortured before his death? The bones of what was left of one of his hands were badly crushed. His former colleagues at the Dugat Automobile Company have informed us that Chambefort had had an accident at home, involving a frying pan that slipped from his grasp and injured one hand. This, at any rate was what he said when he went to ask for sick-leave on 3 or 4 March. He was never seen again.

Having seen a photo of Chambefort's mutilated hand, we venture to maintain that no frying pan, however heavy, could possibly have done so much damage. We should not be surprised to discover that the hand had been crushed in a vice, but that Chambefort, for reasons we may never know, thought it better to pass off the injury as the result of an accident.

The author of the article was Marc Covet. Sensationalism personified.

I threw the paper aside and rang Régine.

The goods news about my health seemed to please her. 'Now,' I said, 'I've a bone to pick with you.'

'I know,' she said.

'You recognized Pierre Brousse the night Yolande was kidnapped, didn't you?'

'Not straight away. But it gradually dawned on me while we were driving along . . .'

'So you made me give up the chase.'

'Yes. I was frightened . . . He always did scare me, somehow. I just couldn't like him.'

'He was a gangster. Maybe you sensed it.'

'Perhaps. But even if the kidnappers had all been strangers, I think I'd still have acted as I did. I was afraid there'd be a fight.'

'I quite understand.'

'The fact that it was Pierre Brousse terrified me even more. With Consuelo just upstairs, I'd lived quite close to him, though he wasn't there all the time. Sometimes we didn't see him for months at a time. But the rue du Dobropol was his base, and I felt sure something terrible was going to happen here. The only way to escape was not to get involved – to pretend I didn't know anything. I hated myself for not telling you.'

'I forgive you,' I said.

'And when you decided to go upstairs to Consuelo's . . .'

'You weren't too keen to join the party.'

'I almost passed out.'

'Maybe Consuelo thought you were putting it on,' I said. 'Inventing an excuse to get away and do something you and I had agreed on before – make a phone-call, for instance.'

'Talking of phones,' said Régine, 'I found that mine had been disconnected. By Consuelo, of course.'

'What else did she do?'

'She put me to bed, and I had a feeling she wasn't going to leave until she was sure I was asleep. But I was so scared I fought to stay awake. I thought maybe she'd poisoned me. Then there were the shots, and she forgot all about me. She listened and listened, then some men went rushing down the stairs, and she left.'

'She went back upstairs,' I said, 'took her suitcase, which she may have prepared beforehand, and hopped it. Perhaps whatever the crooks were looking for was in the case. But even if it wasn't, she couldn't have stayed there any longer.'

'What *were* they looking for?' asked Régine.

'Money, probably,' I said. 'They were part of a gang. They mentioned a man called Sarfotti. Does the name mean anything to you?'

'No.'

'I've heard it somewhere before, but I can't remember where.'

'Not from me, that's for sure.'

'It'll come back to me,' I said. 'So, Consuelo took advantage of your "illness" to put you out of action with her special pick-me-up. My late night visit had aroused her and her boyfriend's suspicions. They must have been keyed up ever since Brousse had broken off with the other two. They were expecting something to go wrong, and they thought I knew more than I did – more than I do even now.'

'So why did they agree to see you?'

'Because Brousse knew a private eye is even more persistent than a regular cop. They reckoned if they didn't let me in, I'd camp on their doorstep, so they thought they might as well take the bull by the horns and find out what I had on my mind. Maybe they hoped they'd be able to fob me off with some tall story or other, and if I didn't cooperate they'd rough me up. They had to get rid of me somehow, because they were just about to fly the coop . . . But let's change the subject. Did you get home all right?'

She said she had. Apparently the block where she lived was in an uproar, but no one had asked her any questions and she hadn't been approached yet by the police.

'If they do come, don't mention me,' I told her, 'even if they say they know I was at Consuelo's. I could easily have gone straight up to her place, without calling on you or anyone else.'

'All right,' she agreed. 'But how would they know you were there?'

'True,' I said. I didn't mention that I'd left my fingerprints all over the place.

'But anyway, you haven't seen me. And you didn't go up there, either. That'll simplify things.'

Before we exchanged affectionate farewells, I asked her whether Brousse might have had occasion to notice the scar on Yolande's thigh. Régine said it was quite possible. There had been parties which ended up very differently from the one last night.

'Tell me,' she said in a choked voice. 'About Yolande . . . ?'

'We'll find her,' I said. 'Don't worry. We'll find her.' And we hung up.

Of course we'd find her. Just as we'd found Chambefort!

At five o'clock Hélène turned up at the doctor's place. 'Congratulations on all your exploits, my wounded hero!' she said sardonically.

'Did you like her?'

'Immensely,' she said. 'And it can't cost much to keep her in clothes. Or should I say out of them?'

Then she grew more serious. 'When are you going to stop frightening the life out of me like that?'

'The day I do that, my love, the Fiat Lux Agency will go broke,' I said.

'Broke?' she said. 'What about this case? You're only working on it out of love for the job – no one's paying you, and all it'll bring in is trouble. Talking of which, Faroux's looking for you. He's called several times, and sent two inspectors round. I told them I'd said goodbye to you at the office last night and hadn't seen you since.'

'He hasn't had you followed, has he?' I said.

'Of course he has. But I didn't come straight here. I shook them off, as they say in the movies.'

Then I brought Hélène up to date on events, and she went back to her theory about the money being from some hold-up.

'Wherever it came from,' I said, 'your gangsters certainly put in a dramatic appearance. Does the Sarfotti gang mean anything to you?'

'No,' she said, 'but we could ask Faroux.'

'Yes, so we could. Or what about Covet? I was forgetting about old Marc. He'll dig that out for us in five minutes.'

I called him at the *Crépu* and, after a few minutes of our usual backchat, managed to slip in my question about Sarfotti.

'Good God!' he cried, suddenly all excited. 'Sarfotti? The bloke with the submarine . . . He and I are practically brothers! . . . And now he's back in the news! . . . Hey, wait a minute! You must be mixed up in that business in the rue du Dobropol!'

'Who told you that?' I said.

'Just my quick wits,' he said. 'It's simple. Faroux's looking for you, and you call me up, sounding cagey, and ask about Sarfotti. Well, just listen . . . A bloke by the name of Pierre Brousse was shot last night in the rue du Dobropol. Only that wasn't his real name. His real name was Pierre Breteau, and he was Sarfotti's right-hand man in Paris. Every police department in the country has been looking for him high and low ever since Sarfotti was arrested!'

'It's coming back to me now,' I said. 'He was the chap who smuggled American cigarettes out of Tangiers to Marseilles or thereabouts, and then had them brought up to be sold around Pigalle. You went and interviewed him in Marseilles, didn't you?'

'That's right,' said Marc. 'Just after he was arrested.'

'What's all this about a submarine?' I asked. 'A real one?'

'Not far off it,' he replied. 'It was an old Greek destroyer he'd had converted. He told me about it when I interviewed him last March.'

Suddenly he grew more agitated still.

'My God, Burma!' he yelled.

If he was excited, what about me? I was bouncing up and down on the bed and almost tearing Hélène's hair out.

'Think of all that happened last March!' he bawled. 'Just in the first few days of last March! Sarfotti was arrested, Chambefort was killed, and Désiris did in his wife and himself. And to crown all, you're the common denominator of the lot! What does it all add up to?'

'Calm down,' I said. 'I'll know what it adds up to when you've answered one more question: when did Sarfotti start using his submarine?'

Marc said he had all the relevant cuttings there in the office. Would I hold on a minute?

'I shan't be able to tell you my conclusions straight away,' I warned him.

'It doesn't matter. I'll wait,' he said.

He must have hurled his phone down. After that, nothing happened for a few minutes. Then he was back again. 'I can't be accurate to within a day, of course . . .'

'Of course.'

'. . . but according to the reports from Marseilles, the submarine's first trips were made in May or June of 1957.'

'Thanks, old sport,' I said. 'Speak to you soon.'

13 Of art and engineering

'That's what it's all about,' I said to Hélène, letting go of her hair. 'One name and one date and everything starts to fall into place.'

'Everything?' Hélène said.

'Almost,' I said. 'Let's recap. Désiris broke the law to get the money he needed to set himself up on the Ile de la Grande-Jatte – just as you thought, my lovely. Only he didn't get it by robbing a bank. He sold his engineering skills to gangsters. His comings and goings from Paris, his resignation from Dugat's, and the first smuggling trip of the "submarine" – they all fit. He went down to the south coast in the middle of February 1957 to convert the old destroyer into a submarine. He may not have worked all on his own, but at any rate he was head of the technical team. He must have been really bright, but like a lot of bright people he just wasn't lucky. He came back to Paris in May or June, loaded with money. Sarfotti was arrested in March 1958, and at about the same time Désiris killed his wife and committed suicide.'

'Just like that!'

'Yes,' I said. 'I tell you, he was unlucky. Chambefort

got hold of his secret designs, and possibly destroyed them. It was just as if the invention had never existed. Désiris decided to get his own back and killed him. That's how matters stood when Sarfotti was nabbed. At which point Désiris thought Sarfotti would talk, and his own involvement with the gang would come to light. That, combined with fear that the Chambefort murder would one day be pinned on him, was too much for him. So he killed himself.'

'But why kill his wife into the bargain?' said Hélène.

'He must have hated her,' I said. 'He'd hoped for so much from her.'

'Especially her money.'

'That's true. And nothing had come of it. So he must have decided to take her with him, hoping her father would die of grief and shame. You remember the note he left on the pillow. "You asked for it!" That was addressed to all the people who'd refused to support his research, and driven him to break the law. The only people who realized how brilliant he was just wanted to exploit him. Only the day before yesterday, Viénot was still hoping to discover the invention and annex it. The gangsters made use of him, too. But they gave him the best deal, when you come to think of it. None of the rest – his father-in-law and his professional colleagues – did anything for him.'

'About the money,' said Hélène. 'If Désiris already had it when he came back to Paris in April 1957, why didn't his wife become suspicious until almost a year later?'

'Either because he started behaving strangely,' I said, 'and she associated it with this money of which she'd never known the source. Or, as I said originally, that was just the excuse she made over the telephone, and what she really wanted me to do was protect her from a man who seemed to have become a stranger.'

'So you've got the whole thing worked out,' said Hélène. 'Amazing what a gunshot wound can do!'

'I'm just trying to account for all the different factors,' I said.

'You could be right,' mused Hélène, 'though there isn't any proof . . . But how the devil did Sarfotti, in Marseilles, dig up exactly the engineer he needed in a factory in Levallois? Someone no one had ever heard of, no matter how brilliant he was?'

'Pierre Brousse must have been the link. Maybe he met Désiris by chance, as he told me, going to buy a car at the factory. They got into conversation, Désiris was desperate for money, and Brousse knew someone looking for a capable engineer. That's all there was to it. Then there was Brousse's party at Consuelo's place, where Désiris met Yolande. The real reason for the celebration must have been the submarine's maiden voyage or something of the sort – "a successful deal," Régine said. Which reminds me – I've a word or two to say to someone else who must have been at that party: Huguette de Mèneval!'

I started to look through the telephone directory.

'It seems too simple to me,' said Hélène, 'their just coming across the very chap they needed, like that. I think it's more likely they knew where to go. They must have found out about Désiris somehow: his difficult situation, his determination to get out of it, and what a brilliant engineer he was.'

'But no one thought he was brilliant!'

'Viénot did,' she said. 'So did Chambefort. And who knows who else?'

'Viénot didn't have anything to do with the gangsters,' I said. 'But you're right about one thing – Brousse can't have met Désiris just by chance.'

The telephone in the rue Rochefort rang long and lugubriously, as though the flat was uninhabited. It was obviously my imagination. There was no reason why the Countess should have moved out.

I hung up.

'No one at home,' I said. 'I'll speak to her another time. I'm in no hurry.'

'What did you want to say to her?' said Hélène.

'I wanted to tell her to stop trying to lead me up the garden, among other things,' I said. 'Her story of the tall man and the short man was a lot of nonsense! She'd recognized at least one of them: Brousse. She must already have met him at Consuelo's.'

'Why should she lie to you?'

'Because she was greedy.'

'The truth didn't cost her anything.'

'No? She must have thought she'd go and tell Brousse there was a private detective after him, but that she hadn't given him away. Then he'd show his gratitude with a nice wad of notes. She'd have kept one of her young friends' boyfriends out of trouble, *and* been paid for it. Not to mention the lolly I'd given her!'

'She was really contemplating a sort of blackmail,' Hélène said.

'Yes. But luckily for her she didn't have time to try it on. Brousse would have knocked her false teeth halfway down her throat.'

'I'm surprised she should contemplate blackmailing one of the men who'd frightened her when they came looking for Yolande!'

'She wasn't frightened!' I laughed. 'She just made

that up to get rid of Yolande when she could no longer pay the rent. The old girl didn't tell Yolande that Brousse was one of the callers, either. If she had, her story wouldn't have held water. It was much simpler just to keep quiet.'

After a short silence, Hélène said slowly: 'That's all very well, but it doesn't throw any more light on what the gangsters were looking for.'

'Money, no doubt. You said so yourself.'

'There must have been a packet of it, then.'

'Yes. Smuggling cigarettes is a very profitable business . . . Désiris and Sarfotti must have kept in touch, even if Brousse did sometimes act as an intermediary. And at some stage Sarfotti may have entrusted Désiris with a fortune to stash away for him.'

'Because Désiris had a clean record,' said Hélène. 'I said that too!'

'Yes. So Sarfotti thought that if anything went wrong, the money would be safe with Désiris. Maybe Sarfotti didn't trust his own gang. And judging by what those two thugs said last night about double-crossing their boss, he was right.'

'Do you think you'll find the money?' she asked.

I shrugged, and got another sharp reminder of the wound beneath my bandages. 'Not any more,' I said. 'Either Désiris hid it so well we'll never track it down, or else he blew it all. It's possible. Keeping Yolande must have been expensive. Anyway, whatever happened to the money, she's the one who paid in the end. When I think how those blockheads believed she could help them! If she'd known where the money was, she wouldn't have been broke!'

'You keep talking about her in the past tense.'

'Let's not kid ourselves.'

Hélène's face fell. 'I suppose not,' she said in a small voice.

Then she roused herself. 'So what do we do now?' she asked.

By way of answer I grabbed the phone and called Marc Covet.

'Splendid!' he said, all of a twitter, when I'd filled him in on the results of my cogitations.

'Maybe,' I said, 'but not for immediate publication. I'm good to you, Covet. You be good to me. I could have kept you in the dark, but I've come clean, so just wait for the moment. I'm not in Faroux's good books at the moment, and I'll need to use what I know to get myself let off the hook. I can't do that if the papers spill the beans beforehand. But don't worry – as soon as I've settled things with Faroux I'll let you know, so even if he does issue a press release, you'll be a day ahead of your competitors.'

'Yes, I know,' said Marc. 'But it's awfully tempting . . .'

'Resist,' I said. 'Look, I'll give you something you can use at once to take the edge off your appetite. Get hold of a photo of Brousse and go and ask Dany Darnys whether he wasn't one of the men who roughed her up last October.'

'But I thought she made all that up.'

'So did I,' I said, 'but she didn't. It all fits together, my friend!'

I hung up.

'And now?' said Hélène.

'The case is closed,' I said. 'The best thing for me to do now is go and see Faroux and let him tear me off a strip.'

'Right away?' she said.

'No,' I said. 'In a day or so. The doc says I'll be up and about by tomorrow.'

'Good. But meanwhile you must get some rest.' And she started trying to tuck me in.

'None of that!' I said, swinging my legs to the floor. 'I've got to get out of here! The cops are going to question Régine. I've told her to keep quiet, but she won't stand up to a tough interrogation. So they'll probably turn up here in a few hours at the most.'

'But where do you mean to go?' she said. 'There's no question of going to your place. And mine's no better. We can't go to the office, and as for a hotel . . .'

'We'll think about that later,' I said. 'Now go and get the doc.'

I strode around the room in my shirt tails as I waited. When he came in I told him I intended to leave. He asked me how I felt, and I said as hangovers went, this one wasn't too bad. He said the good thing about being an alcoholic was that you could always remember having felt worse. Then he examined me and said he thought I was all right. I still had a bit of a temperature, but that was probably only because Hélène was there. I ought to be able to take the air without any ill effects.

'I'll put a fresh dressing on that wound, all the same,' he said. 'And if you feel seedy – ' handing me a tube of pills ' – take two of these in a glass of water.'

'I'm hungry,' I said. 'Am I allowed to eat?'

'No reason why not,' he said. 'But not too much. There's all you need in the kitchen.'

He changed the dressing and Hélène rustled up some dinner. By then it was nine o'clock. Time to go.

A chill wind was blowing out in the avenue de Neuilly. The pavement, damp from the drizzle, gleamed under the street lamps. I felt a bit giddy, but it wasn't too bad. Hélène was still wondering where I meant to go.

I hailed a passing taxi.

'The corner of the rue de Prony and the rue Rochefort,' I told the driver.

'What . . . ?' Hélène began as we moved off.

'I'm going to ask the Countess to take us in,' I said.

'My God!' she wailed. 'And the doctor said the fever had subsided!'

The rear light of the taxi disappeared into the night. We started down the rue Rochefort like a pair of adulterers heading for a hired love-nest. We passed a couple of furtive-looking pedestrians – perhaps on their way out of some similar haven. There was a line of cars parked along the kerb. Zavatter was in one of them, sitting at the wheel.

'Hi!' I said. 'You certainly earn your money! I didn't think you'd still be here. Are you going to stay all night?'

'I'm still here because I have a feeling something's wrong,' he told me, nodding in the direction of the Countess's place.

Hélène asked if that was where we were going. I said it was.

Beyond the garden wall and the trees, chinks of light were visible between the ground-floor curtains of the house that was once the scene of Désiris's guilty amours. Everything was amazingly quiet. Cars kept sweeping past both ends of the street, but here a discreet silence reigned.

'It looks very posh,' said Hélène.

'And she got it all lying flat on her back,' I said.

'What makes you think there's something fishy going on, Zavatter?'

'Get in the car,' he said, 'and I'll explain.'

He told us he'd started watching the house immediately after my call the evening before, at around six. Huguette had come out a little after seven and gone on foot to a bookshop in the rue de Courcelles. It had just closed, but she insisted on the bloke opening up again. She'd come out of the shop with a hefty tome under her arm, and gone straight home. Zavatter waited till all the lights were out in the house, then left, at about nine. He was back at nine this morning, just in time to see the maid getting into a taxi with a suitcase. Since then, nothing.

'No one's gone in and no one's come out,' he said. 'And at this time yesterday, all the lights were out. There's something funny going on.'

'Well, she's not very steady on her pins,' I said. 'She must often just stay at home. It must have been a struggle for her to get to the bookshop.'

'Yes,' said Zavatter. 'She must really have wanted the book.'

'That's not impossible,' I said. 'It's not that that's worrying me. Are you sure she hasn't been out since?'

'Certain.'

'Because I called her today, at about . . .'

'Half-past six,' said the efficient Hélène.

'And there was no answer,' said I.

'The lights were on at half-past six!' said Zavatter.

'Maybe she never answers the phone,' Hélène suggested, without much conviction.

'Stay there,' I said, 'and keep your eye on the windows.'

I got out of the car and went and rang the bell. The sound shattered the silence, faded, and died away. No reaction. I tried the gate, just in case. Shut. I tried the bell again, again without success, then rejoined my assistants.

'What happened to the lights?' I said.

'Nothing.'

I lit my pipe.

'We have to get to the bottom of this, Zav,' I said. 'Drop us at a café, then go and fetch something we can use to pick a lock.'

From the back seat there came a mocking chuckle.

'So the case is closed, is it?'

I called up several more times from the café where Zavatter left us, letting the phone ring until it must have been red-hot. But still no one answered. Zavatter came back after about an hour with the wherewithal for a break-in, and we went back to the rue Rochefort.

The lights were still on in the groundfloor windows, and while Zavatter set to work on the gate, Hélène and I played the young lovers and loitered about on the pavement, keeping watch. Shortly afterwards we were inside. The crunching of the gravel path under our feet was deafening, but we threw caution to the winds and walked straight on. If Huguette de Mèneval loomed up and objected to our visit, we could say we'd given her enough warning. But she didn't loom up, and we made our way into the drawing-room where she'd received me the day before.

The seductive smile of Archet's Mademoiselle de Mèneval looked down on the scene. A lamp with an enormous shade stood on the grand piano, casting dim rays on all the bric-à-brac. There was no one there.

The ill-assorted furniture seemed frozen in an attitude of anxious expectancy, with each table or chair trying to hide in its neighbour's shadow. An open book lay open on a reading stand, awaiting the reader's return. Why did everything seem to be silently waiting and watching? I picked up the book.

It was open at a full-page picture of a bearded man. Frédéric Langlat. The painter. The first owner of the house. I looked at the title. *Artistic Curiosities of the XVIIth Arrondissement*. The old girl had been doing her homework on the neighbourhood, no doubt so as to be able to impress people. I put the book back on the stand and wondered if we shouldn't try to let someone know we were there.

'Is there anybody at home?' squeaked Hélène as if she'd read my mind. But her voice was smothered in all the clutter of furniture. There wasn't even an echo. Zavatter gave a nervous cough.

It was time to explore the Sleeping Beauty's castle. For a start we went up to the first floor, where Desiris's and Yolande's territory once began. And there at last, in the room directly underneath the artist's studio, we found Huguette de Mèneval.

She wouldn't wind anyone else around her little finger.

Because, for one thing, she was dead. It didn't surprise me, really.

But there was another thing. And that did surprise me.

One of the corpse's hands was terribly crushed.

14 Truth dawns

'Good grief!' gasped Zavatter.

'My God!' moaned Hélène, backing into a chair and collapsing on to it.

I didn't say anything.

My eyes were moving slowly from that bloody hand to a stepladder that had fallen over, and then up the wall. There was a snake-like trickle of some unpleasant substance on the reddish tapestry. Red on red, but the stain was the darker. It seemed to be coming from the angle where wall and ceiling met.

It was only then that my eyes returned to the body and I noticed what looked like pebbles of some kind, varying in size, scattered about by the body. The torn pouch they must have come from was lying near by. Then certain aspects of the corpse caught my attention: the old-fashioned ankle-boots; the darned black silk stocking drawn on over varicose veins; grotesque layers of petticoat. My eyes lingered on the dishevelled bleached hair, sticking out in all directions as if the old woman had seen a ghost. The face had gone terribly blue beneath its make-up, and the eyes were protruding. Then I looked at the hand again . . . the overturned stepladder . . . the trail of red winding up the wall to the ceiling.

Frédéric Langlat looked down at the scene from his frame, brush in hand. The day before, there had been another little painting hanging on the wall beside the self-portrait. Now the smaller picture was lying on the floor, and in its place was a small sliding door, at present open wide. I looked inside and saw a complex-looking mechanism consisting of a spring, some cogs and a few connecting rods. Désiris could have knocked it up in five minutes. There was a handle just asking to be pulled. When I did so there was a click and an almost imperceptible hum.

'Well, I'll be damned!' said Zavatter.

I looked up. The ceiling was rolling aside on invisible hinges, opening up a gap more than a foot wide between it and the top of the red-tapestried wall. Another click, and both humming and movement stopped.

'Well, I'll be damned!' said Zavatter again.

Artistic Curiosities of the XVIIth Arrondissement. It must contain some really interesting little mysteries.

As I gazed at the gap in the ceiling, I remembered hearing about another painter, contemporary with Langlat, who liked working on very large canvases and who installed a contraption that wound them up from under his studio floor a bit at a time, so that he could operate on whatever part he chose of his current picture, and then wind it down again. Langlat must have liked daubing on the grand scale, too, and included a similar mechanism in the plans of this house.

While all this was going through my mind, Zavatter had gone over by the wall and was playing his torch around the gap in the ceiling.

'There's a cavity up there,' he said.

'I'm sure there is,' I said. 'It's the hiding-place.'

He righted the stepladder and started climbing up it.

'Look out!' I shouted.

There was no warning click. The ceiling just snapped back into place, striking the wall with a loud crash.

'Well, I'll be damned!' Zavatter let out a yell this time.

'It's either a fault in the mechanism or a trap,' I said. 'The latter, in my opinion.'

Hélène, though she still couldn't look at the body, was no longer terrified. There was a glint in her eye.

'So that's how Chambefort hurt his hand,' she said. 'He must have done it when he stole Désiris's designs.'

'Yes,' I said. 'The only difference between Chambefort and the Countess was that he was young enough to stand the shock, and was bumped off later, whereas the Countess was old and had a heart condition. It's my fault in a way. If I hadn't hinted there might be some money hidden in the house, to get my own back for the yarns she'd spun me, she would never have started looking.'

I picked up the pouch, fixed the tear with a pin, and began picking up the pebbles scattered around on the floor. Zavatter helped me. Hélène looked on.

'Anyway,' I said, 'thanks to her we've found the treasure that Sarfotti gave Désiris to look after. The treasure all the crooks were after.'

'What is it exactly?' asked Hélène, though she had a very good idea of the answer.

'Contraband,' I said. 'Sarfotti's speciality. But not cigarettes! Uncut diamonds. It's not a very big bag, is it? But even with the dealer's cut, the costs of polishing, and perhaps a bit of wastage, I'll bet there are several million francs worth of stones here.'

It was raining. Outside, the wind howled round the house and through the trees in the garden, driving gusts of rain against the drawing-room windows. Every so often the brass hood over the fireplace rattled.

Inside, I sat listening. I was alone with the portrait of Mademoiselle de Mèneval on the wall, with the real-life, or rather real-death, version lying upstairs. Also present: the book on the artistic curiosities of the XVIIth arrondissement, and the diamonds.

I'd declined to leave with Zavatter and Hélène. Hélène said I was mad, but I'd explained I was fine here. The central heating was on, there were plenty of comfortable chairs and settees. And I wasn't likely to be disturbed. We'd been all over the house, and deduced that the maid had been given a holiday – so that her mistress could carry out her search in peace – and had gone off to the country. Faroux must be dying to get his hands on me, but he'd never come looking for me here.

I'd see him, but I'd see him when I chose. I had no intention of being picked up tonight with the bag of stones in my pocket. There'd be a watch on my flat, and on Hélène's and Zavatter's as well, and hotels weren't safe. So for the time being I was going to stay put and get a bit of rest.

Of course I could have thought of more exciting company than the Countess, but I preferred sleeping here with a harmless corpse upstairs to sitting at police headquarters with a lamp shining into my eyes and coppers blowing cigarette smoke all over me.

No. I wasn't as mad as Hélène thought. And anyway there was something I had to do.

I'd shaken some of the diamonds out on to a table, and now I began to toy with them idly. Some of them were dull all over their surfaces and looked like ordinary stones, the sort that couldn't hurt a fly unless launched with a catapult. But these were no ordinary stones: dull as they looked, they were as lethal as the rest. Some of the rest had cracks in their surfaces, and gave off strange lights as they moved. A number of these gleams were green. Emeralds. Like the one Yolande wore on her finger. Désiris had given her a gift fit for a princess, but it hadn't cost him much. Just the jeweller's fee for cutting it. They say emeralds bring bad luck. Probably a fiction thought up by people who owned emeralds to put off people who didn't. But Yolande's had got her into trouble with Brousse and company. They thought it meant she knew where the rest were stowed.

I hunted round for something to put the pouchful of diamonds in, and quickly found what I was looking for: a small old-fashioned carpet-bag.

Shortly afterwards I turned out the light and lay down on the sofa near the radiator. And despite the wind and the rain, now redoubled in violence, despite the brooding shapes of the furniture all around me; despite the dead body upstairs – I went to sleep as peacefully as a child, happy in the knowledge of a job well done.

I was jolted awake by the telephone. It was echoing through the house with menacing insistence. Throwing off my overcoat, which I'd been using as a blanket, I stood up and looked at the luminous dial of my watch. Two o'clock. Who could be ringing Huguette de Mèneval at this hour? She couldn't be listed as a call-girl! I counted the number of rings as they jangled in my brain. Fifteen. Then whoever it was gave up.

I sat down again and waited in the darkness, listening. The wind had dropped but the rain still thudded down monotonously. Somewhere a gutter gurgled.

The telephone was a nice, friendly invention, I told myself. Everyone was familiar with it. It was meant to ring at any time of the day or night. There was nothing extraordinary about what had just happened. So why was my heart beating so fast? Why was I having difficulty breathing?

A few minutes passed, and then it rang again. I jumped, even though I'd been expecting it. Twenty rings this time. Then a short pause. Then it started again. This time it went on, with one or two interruptions, for about half an hour. After which, nothing. Nothing but the lullaby of the rain and an occasional creak from the furniture. I lay down again, but didn't sleep. I was brought upright again by the violent jangling of the street-door bell.

Silence. Oppressive. Almost tangible.

I had a fair idea of what was going to happen next. I wrapped up the bag with the diamonds in it in my coat, and stuffed the whole lot under the sofa. Then I crept quietly among the sideboards and wardrobes, thanking my lucky stars for the cover they offered, and selected a hiding place well away from all the doors. Then I kept absolutely still, all my senses alert, and waited.

But not for long.

A door opened and closed again. Voices whispered. A torch started playing over the walls. Then the lamp on the piano was switched on. I couldn't see anything from where I was, but I couldn't be seen either.

'What a shambles!' said one of the mysterious visitors. He sounded tense, and had an accent difficult to place, which he seemed to be trying to conceal. 'What do you think the old girl's up to? At her age she can't still be staying out all night!'

'I think she's here,' said a second voice. 'She must be asleep. She probably has insomnia, like all old people, and guzzles sleeping pills. It takes a bomb to wake them up.'

I shuddered. It would take more than a bomb to wake this one up.

'Keep your medical lectures for another day,' said the one with the accent, sarcastically.

'All right, Sarfotti – keep your hair on!' grumbled his companion.

Sarfotti!

Wonders would never cease! He must have escaped from prison recently, and the cops were keeping it quiet for tactical reasons. Désiris must have told him where the stones were hidden, and now he'd come back to pick them up. He was in for a disappointment.

'Let's make sure about the old woman,' he said.

The two of them went out of the room without switching off the lamp, but were back almost immediately.

'She must be out on the town,' said the smuggler. 'We'd better get a move on. She might come back at any minute. Now, let's see – when I came here with Désiris he took me up some outstairs steps and in through a side door on the first floor. But these stairs must lead up there too. Come on!'

Shortly afterwards I heard loud exclamations of surprise from upstairs. They'd found Huguette. Nothing happened for a while, then a dull, almost imperceptible humming broke the silence. If I hadn't already heard it I wouldn't have picked it up, even though all my senses were on the alert. I waited for a cry of pain. Nothing. Désiris had told Sarfotti how the system worked.

Then they were back again.

'Good God! Did you see that?' said Sarfotti. 'Did you? I can't make it out!'

A chair scraped on the floor. He must have sat down to get over the shock.

'There's one thing I *can* make out,' his friend said cuttingly. 'If you'd handed the stuff over to me instead of to that bastard—'

'I thought it was safe,' said Sarfotti, 'because Désiris was a respectable citizen.'

'I thought so too,' said the other.

'And I liked him.'

'Yeah. A real darling!' the second spat out.

'I mean it,' said Sarfotti. 'I trusted him – ' he paused significantly – 'more than I do you.'

'You didn't have any choice,' muttered the other bitterly.

'And I was wondering . . .' Sarfotti went on.

Then I heard him stand up.

'You'd better not be trying to bloody-well double-cross me!' he hissed.

'What are you talking about?' said his companion. 'Haven't I been putting you up ever since you escaped?'

'Maybe *you* didn't have any choice! And perhaps you're just waiting for me to drop my guard.'

'Don't talk rubbish!'

Sarfotti let off another volley of oaths and then said: 'I don't like this business about the key. Oh, it's no good gaping at me. I'm not daft, you know. The key to the outside door, I mean. I don't give a damn how you got it, but the fact is you did, and the stones have disappeared. And I thought nobody knew I had them. At any rate, nobody knew I'd passed them on to Désiris except Angèle.'

Angèle? Who the hell was she? Sarfotti's voice had gone husky when he mentioned her. Well, who was I to complain if there was another dame in the picture?

'And even Angèle didn't know where the hiding-place was,' Sarfotti went on. 'I don't know who the bastards were that tortured her last March. Probably the same ones that got Brousse. And I don't know whether she talked. But anyway there must have been some sort of leak, and they already knew I had the diamonds, otherwise they wouldn't have tackled her. So who's to say you didn't get wind of something, too? You had the key. All you had to do was come here and find the hiding-place. The old girl found it, even if the stones had gone by the time she got there. And who'd taken them? Can you tell me that?'

'Calm down, for God's sake,' said the other one soothingly. But there was more than a hint of fear in his voice.

After a silence Sarfotti growled: 'Let's go and talk about it at your place. But if you've double-crossed me . . .' He swore in what sounded like a Corsican dialect, and their informative discussion ceased.

The light went out. A door slammed. There were hurried footsteps on the gravel path outside.

Unless I'd imagined it. And imagined, too, the roar of a car engine starting up. There were so many sounds echoing in my brain.

After a moment I got up and squeezed out from between the sideboard and the armchair, where I'd been crouched all this time. I took a few hesitant steps in the darkness, knocking into the furniture. I had so little feeling in my legs it was like coming round after being knocked out. I got as far as the telephone, put my hand on it, then paused. I listened to the music of the rain outside.

After all, it could wait. I'd learnt a lot from Sarfotti's visit, but my plan was still unchanged.

I went back to the sofa and lay down. Alone again, except for the thoughts jostling around in my brain.

15 Full circle

Sunday, 9 November. Seven p.m. It was still raining. And my head was still sore, but I'd allowed myself a pipe. The smoke mingled with the two clouds issuing from Superintendent Faroux's nostrils as he sat opposite me.

I'd had a job getting hold of him. I'd been at it since waking up in the Countess's old curiosity shop at ten o'clock that morning. No wonder the cops couldn't solve their cases if all the blokes they were after had as much trouble as I did turning themselves in. Faroux hadn't been either at home or in his office. He'd been out on some investigation at the back of beyond, and no one had known when he'd be back. I'd called more times than you could count on the fingers of any number of crushed hands, and had got him at last at about five o'clock in the afternoon.

'Hello, Faroux? Burma here. I believe you're looking for me.'

'What makes you think that?'

'That's right, play for time while one of your pals finds out where I'm calling from! You cops have to try to be clever even on Sundays. Well, I'll tell you why I thought you might be looking for me. Because you found my visiting card at the scene of a violent crime in the rue du Dobropol, not to mention a smashed whisky glass with my prints on it, and my car parked in the street outside.'

'That's right. But also because you witnessed the Mège girl's kidnapping, and were taken to see a doctor friend of yours by a certain Régine Monteuil after you'd stopped a bullet. And so forth. Do we agree?'

'Yes. And I hope we'll go on doing so. I want to make a statement.'

Hélène had come with me to police headquarters, where Fabre pretended to think the carpet-bag contained a change of clothes to take to gaol with me. And I'd told Faroux about everything – everything except my spade work on the Ile de la Grande-Jatte and what had happened the night before in the rue Rochefort. Now we were sitting looking at each other like two oracles, our smoke rings mingling in the air above us.

The super cleared his throat, extracted some brand-new shiny photographs from a file, and held them out to me.

'If you'd got in touch with us before, instead of trying to do it all on your own, things might have been different,' he said. 'Here are the results.'

I didn't answer. I just looked down at the photographs. Yolande Mège. She didn't have much on, as usual. But these pictures hadn't been taken for *Purely Parisian Thrills*.

'She was fished out of the Seine this morning,' said Faroux. 'I've been out there all day. A nice way to spend a Sunday.'

I didn't ask him whereabouts in the Seine. What

difference did it make? I tried to clear my throat.

'What are all those black marks on the body?' I said.

'Those blokes get their cigarettes cheap,' said Faroux. 'They probably got through several packets in that place on the Ile de la Grande-Jatte. We found a scarf there that may have belonged to her. Several packets,' he said again. 'Cigarettes are their speciality.'

Hélène shuddered and drew her coat around her more tightly.

Faroux flicked his cigarette butt into the ashtray.

'Here's another example of their handywork,' he said disgustedly, handing me some more photos. They were of a woman I'd never seen before, half-naked like Yolande, her skin dotted with burns.

'Angèle Varlet,' said Faroux. 'Sarfotti's mistress in Paris. But we didn't know that until this happened.'

'Last March, wasn't it?' I said. 'It was in the papers.'

Faroux nodded.

'She must have known Sarfotti had left something in Désiris's safe-keeping.' I said. 'And it was the thugs I saw in the rue de Dobropol who'd tortured her and made her talk. It didn't get them far, though. Désiris was dead, but they couldn't search his place: even though you'd called it suicide and buried the case along with the body, they may have thought that that was just a front, and that the house in the rue Alphonse-de-Neuville was being watched. So they lay low for a few months, until Brousse, who'd been doing the same, turned up at Consuelo's place again. They thought he might be useful to them, made contact, and offered him a cut in return for what he knew. He must have told them Yolande had information, and that explains the whole chain of events. The visits to Huguette de

Mèneval, to Dany Darnys, whom they took to be Yolande, and all the rest of it. They lay low again after the Darnys fiasco, probably not believing what the papers said about the attack being taken as a hoax, and surfaced again when Consuelo told them Yolande was back from the south. We know what happened next. But they made another big mistake. They thought a certain detail proved that Yolande knew everything.'

'What detail was that?' said Faroux impatiently.

'A stone in a ring,' I said.

'A stone in a ring? What was it they were really after, then?'

'This,' I said.

I stood up, took the pouch of diamonds from the famous bag, and shook them out in front of him.

'*Les jeux sont faits,*' I said. '*Rien ne va plus*. Around three million on the table.'

Jaws dropped.

'Where did you get hold of them?' said Faroux.

I sat down again.

'In the false ceiling of a house in the rue Rochefort,' I said. And added a brief explanation.

'Three million, eh?' Faroux mused. 'It was worth killing three people for that much!'

'Four,' I said.

'Four? Oh, you mean Chambefort!'

'No, old chap,' I said. 'It wasn't the diamonds that got him. It was the invention. And notice I say "invention" and not "inventor". Désiris didn't kill him.'

Faroux gave a start. 'How do you know that?' he said. 'It hasn't been released to the press yet.'

'Just a hunch,' I said. 'So it's true.'

'Quite true. Chambefort went to have his hand

treated in hospital shortly before he was killed. Désiris had been dead for several days by then. The hospital records prove it.'

He frowned. 'Do you know who did kill him?'

'I think so, yes,' I said. 'I'll tell you later. But first, about the fourth murder victim. It was Huguette de Mèneval.'

I told him what had happened during the first part of the previous night.

'The hand!' he said. 'So Chambefort too must have . . .'

'Found the moving ceiling, yes,' I said. 'It couldn't have been used for ages. It had dwindled into a kind of legend. Even the Countess had only heard of it vaguely, if at all, until I got her worked up the other evening talking about money, and then she started racking her brains.'

'Someone else who must be pleased to have come across you and your sense of humour,' said Faroux.

I ignored that remark and went on: 'Désiris pressed the ceiling into service again – unbeknownst to everyone, including Yolande – as a hiding-place for the secret elements of his invention. He – and Chambefort too – must have learned of its existence from one of the various books on the area. Anyone can get hold of them. There's something about the contraption in this book, which Mme de Mèneval bought the other evening.'

I took *Artistic Curiosities of the XVIIth Arrondissement* from the bag and laid it down beside the diamonds.

Faroux turned to Inspector Fabre. 'Wasn't there a book like this at Chambefort's place?' he said.

'Yes, monsieur,' Fabre said. 'Exactly the same one.'

'Right,' I said. 'Chambefort visited the house on 2 or 3 March, when there was no one there, not even the maid.'

'Broke in, you mean?' said Faroux.

'No, he had a key,' I said. 'Bear that in mind, because that key unlocks the whole mystery. It was one he'd copied or had copied from an impression he'd made of the lock on the street door. That's the door that counts. You can always manage the others, always assuming they're not already unlocked. You know what happened next, except that he didn't take the diamonds – he was only interested in the papers, and didn't even bother to look inside the pouch. Désiris got back to find the plans gone and traces of blood in the room, which he washed off with the first thing he could lay his hands on: some shirts he then threw in with the dirty laundry. He was in a terrible rage, understandably, not knowing whom to suspect, and because of the house having been left empty. Maybe he hadn't made a copy of the plans. Anyway, even if he had, it was soon put out of his mind when he found out Sarfotti had been arrested. The various blows, one after the other, were too much for him. He thought he was doomed to disaster, and one really might say he killed himself and his wife in a fit of madness.'

'No doubt,' said Faroux. 'But to go back to Chambefort. He still managed to get himself bumped off on the Ile de la Grande-Jatte. It wasn't Désiris who killed him, so who was it?'

'I'm coming to that,' I said.

'And what about this key that unlocks everything?'

'That, too,' I said. 'What did you find in Chambefort's pockets?'

'A penknife, some change, and some half-disintegrated papers we managed to piece together to identify him. Nothing else . . . Ah! No keys! Is that what you're getting at? . . . No keys at all.'

'So the bloke who killed him . . .' I said. 'Oh, by the way – how was he killed?'

'Shot twice,' said Faroux. 'The doctor dug out the bullets.'

'So the assassin pinched his keys. The key to where Chambefort lived, so he could go and do a bit of prospecting, and the one to Huguette de Mèneval's outer door.'

I now told him what had happened during the second part of the previous night. When I said one of men was Sarfotti, Faroux nearly went through the roof.

'Good God, Burma! And you let him escape?'

'Hold on,' I said. 'I'm not a copper.'

'That's enough fooling around!' Faroux bellowed, as if we'd been playing games for the last hour. 'I want to know what they said and did, and I want to know all of it! Maybe it'll give us a clue. And no more strokes of genius like magic keys. Sarfotti can't have killed Chambefort. He was locked up in Marseilles at the time.'

'I'm not accusing Sarfotti,' I said. 'It was the other bloke who had the key, so he was the one that killed Chambefort . . . And if it's of any interest, Sarfotti's staying at his house. You can pick him up there whenever you like.'

'But who is he?' shouted Faroux.

I held out a handkerchief.

'Take this,' I said. 'You'll be even hotter in a minute. He's no small-time crook. He's a respectable citizen to all appearances, a businessman. Not too scrupulous perhaps, but how many business men are? He didn't like Désiris, but when Sarfotti had the idea of the submarine he recommended Désiris all the same. He knew he was good at his job, and he knew he'd accept, because he needed money. After that, he had Chambefort shadow every move Désiris made in the hope of getting his hands on the invention. I don't know why he killed Chambefort later on – maybe because Chambefort wanted to keep the invention all to himself – but I'm sure he'll be only too delighted to tell you. Anyway he took the keys off Chambefort's body, and when Sarfotti, who'd turned up at his place, said he wanted to get into Désiris's apartment to find some diamonds, all our friend had to do was produce the relevant key. He must have regretted not knowing about the diamonds earlier, all the same. So off they went in the wind and rain of a cold November night to—'

'That'll do!' bawled Faroux. 'You're not writing some trashy novel! What's his name?'

'His name is Auguste André Labouchère, and he lives in the avenue de la Grande-Armée. He was Désiris's father-in-law.'

Faroux did need my handkerchief now to mop his brow. They could all have done with one.

When I got to the office at about three the following afternoon, Hélène was waiting impatiently.

'Well?' she said.

'They nabbed them both this morning,' I said. 'Sarfotti and Labouchère. The old man's making a confession at this moment. A real nutter. Sarfotti's keeping his mouth shut – he thinks it was the nutter who shopped him. Labouchère has been mixed up with crooks for years, but he dreamed of a brilliant match for his daughter. More brilliant than Désiris, whom he hated for being poor and for having wormed his way into the family. But he found out what a good engineer he was, and introduced him to Sarfotti so that the smuggling operation would be more profitable, and also so as to compromise him.'

'That's what caused his death, in a way,' said Hélène.

'Yes,' I said. 'Désiris was working for his father-in-law without knowing it. He came back loaded with Sarfotti's money, and set himself up on the Ile de la Grande-Jatte. And it was then, according to Labouchère's statement, that Chambefort, perhaps because he was jealous of Désiris, came and offered Labouchère his services as a spy. Labouchère doesn't deny killing Chambefort. He'd have a hard time doing that. The police found the revolver at his house. He says Chambefort got his just deserts. He claims he'd got hold of the plans, and that he set fire to them while Labouchère looked on. It so incensed him he couldn't control himself.'

'That's obviously not true,' said Hélène.

'Of course not,' I said.

'How did it happen, then?'

'Labouchère arranged to meet Chambefort at the workshop, intending to get the plans back and then eliminate him.'

'So Chambefort didn't give them to him as soon as he'd stolen them?'

'No. He was too badly hurt. He obviously hid them again while he went to get his hand treated, and came to the appointment in the workshop when it was more or less healed. Then he must have smelt a rat and chucked the plans into the stove. We know the rest.'

'Tell me,' said Hélène after a short silence, 'why did he call you round to his house after his daughter's death?'

'He was worried,' I said. 'He wanted to know how much I knew, where I fitted into the picture, exactly what his daughter had said to me. He really harped on that. And now I know why. He was afraid she'd suspected something about him and Désiris, and had already told me too much.'

'And had she?'

'She hadn't told me a thing. But maybe he didn't believe that. We'll never know.'

'What about Brousse's killers?'

'Faroux's hoping they'll try and sell Yolande's emerald, and he'll nab them that way. It won't have been their lucky stone, either.'

'And Consuelo?'

'Vanished without trace.'

'And what about you? How's that wound?'

'OK. And now the party's over, I'll be able to rest without feeling guilty.'

'Yes,' she sighed. 'I'm really glad the horrible business is finished. I shan't forget this case in a hurry . . . By the way, I'm not unduly interested in money, but how much cash did you get out of it?'

'None,' I said, laughing. 'But I'll tell you how many expenses if you like.' And I began counting up on my fingers.

'Not to mention that bullet-hole,' she reminded me. 'And even your friend Régine's lost her job since you gave her boss a purely Parisian punch on the nose.'

'So much the better,' I said. 'It was an immoral way of earning a living, anyway. I'm all in favour of morality. The wicked ought to be punished and the virtuous ought to be rewarded.'

And before she could stop me I'd twitched the neck of her dress and dropped something down the front. She shrieked and pushed me away.

'What have you put in my . . .' she began, plunging her hand inside her bra.

'You'll soon see,' I said. 'Unless you'd like me to get it out for you.'

She found the object in question and brought it forth into the light of day.

'My God!' she whispered. 'A diamond.'

'It's yours,' I said. 'You've earned it. And there are two more where that came from.'

I took them out of my pocket and put them on the desk. 'One for Régine, and one for yours truly.'

'But how did you . . .'

'You remember the carpet-bag?'

'Yes?'

'Well, it was padded inside, and somehow or other these three sparklers slipped down into the lining. Funny thing, eh?'